THE PAPER MOON

Also by Andrea Camilleri

ANDREA CAMILLERI

THE PAPER MOON

Translated by Stephen Sartarelli

PICADOR

First published 2008 by Penguin Books,
a member of Penguin Group (USA) Inc., New York

This hardback edition first published in Great Britain 2008 by Picador
an imprint of Pan Macmillan Ltd
Pan Macmillan, 20 New Wharf Road, London N1 9RR
Basingstoke and Oxford
Associated companies throughout the world
www.panmacmillan.com

ISBN 978-0-330-45727-9

Copyright © Sellerio Editore 2005
Translation copyright © Stephen Sartarelli 2008

Originally published in Italian as *La luna di carta* by Sellerio Editore, Palermo.

The right of Andrea Camilleri to be identified as the
author of this work has been asserted by him in accordance
with the Copyright, Designs and Patents Act 1988.

1 3 5 7 9 8 6 4 2

A CIP catalogue record for this book is available from
the British Library.

Typeset by SetSystems Ltd, Saffron Walden, Essex
Printed and bound in Great Britain by
Mackays of Chatham plc, Chatham, Kent

Visit **www.picador.com** to read more about all our books
and to buy them. You will also find features, author interviews and
news of any author events, and you can sign up for e-newsletters
so that you're always first to hear about our new releases.

THE PAPER MOON

1

The alarm rang, as it had done every morning for the past year, at seven thirty. But he had woken up a fraction of a second before the bell; the release of the spring that set off the ringing had sufficed. He therefore had time, before jumping out of bed, to look at the window and realize, from the light, that the day promised to be a fine one, without clouds. Afterwards he just barely had time to make coffee, drink a cup, do what he needed to do, shave and shower, drink another cup, fire up a cigarette, get dressed, go outside, get into his car and pull up at the station at nine — all at the slapstick speed of Larry Semon or Charlie Chaplin.

Until a year earlier, his morning wake-up routine had followed different rules and, most of all, there was no rush, no hundred-yard dashes.

First, no alarm clock.

Montalbano was in the habit of opening his eyes naturally after a night's sleep, with no need of external stimuli.

He did have an alarm clock of sorts, but it was inside him, buried somewhere in his brain. He merely had to set it before falling asleep, telling himself, 'Don't forget you have to get up tomorrow at six,' and the next morning his eyes would pop open at six o'clock sharp. He'd always considered the alarm clock, the metal kind, a sort of instrument of torture. The three or four times he'd had to use that drill-like noise to wake up – because Livia, who had to leave the next morning, didn't trust his inner alarm – he'd spent the rest of the day with a headache. Then Livia, after a squabble, had bought a plastic alarm clock that instead of ringing made an electronic sound, a kind of unending *beeeeeep*, rather like a little fly that had found its way into your ear and got stuck inside. Enough to drive you crazy. He'd ended up throwing it out of the window, which had set off another memorable spat.

Second, he would wake himself up, intentionally, a bit earlier than necessary, some ten minutes earlier at the very least.

These were the best ten minutes of the day ahead. Ah, how wonderful it was to lie in bed, under the covers, thinking of idiocies! Should I buy that book everybody's calling a masterpiece or not? Should I eat out today, or come home and bolt down what Adelina's prepared for me? Should I or shouldn't I tell Livia that I can't wear the shoes she bought me because they're too tight? That sort of thing. Poking about with the mind. While carefully avoiding any thought of sex or women. That could be dangerous terrain at such an hour, unless Livia was there sleeping beside him, ready and happy to face the consequences.

One morning a year earlier, however, things had suddenly changed. He had barely opened his eyes, calculating that he had a scant fifteen minutes to devote to his mental dawdlings, when a thought – not a whole one, but the start of one – came into his mind, and it began with these exact words: When your dying day comes . . .

What was this thought doing there with the others? How gutless! It was like suddenly remembering, while making love, that he hadn't paid the phone bill. Not that he was inordinately frightened by the idea of dying; the problem was that six thirty in the morning was hardly the proper time and place for it. If one started thinking about death at the crack of dawn, certainly by five in the afternoon one would either shoot oneself or jump into the sea with a rock round one's neck. He managed to prevent that phrase proceeding any further, blocking its path by counting very fast from one to five thousand, with eyes shut and fists clenched. Then he realized that the only solution was to set about doing the things he needed to do, concentrating on them as though it were a matter of life or death. The following morning was even more treacherous. The first thought that entered his mind was that the fish soup he'd eaten the night before had lacked some seasoning. But which? And at that exact moment the same ghastly thought came back to him: When your dying day comes . . .

As of then, he had understood that the thought would never go away. It might very well lie buried deep inside some curlicue in his brain for a day or two only to pop back out into the open when he least expected it. For no reason, he became convinced that his very survival depended on preventing that sentence ever completing itself. For if it did, he would die when the last word came.

Hence the alarm clock. To leave not even the slightest fissure in time for that accursed thought to slip through.

When she came to spend three days in Vigàta, Livia, as she was unpacking, pointed at the bedside table and asked: 'What's that alarm doing there?'

He answered with a lie. 'Well, a week ago I had to get up really early and—'

'And a week later it's still set?'

When she put her mind to it, Livia was worse than Sherlock Holmes. Embarrassed, he told her the truth, the whole truth, and nothing but the truth.

Livia burst out: 'You're demented!' And she buried the alarm clock in a drawer inside the armoire.

The following morning it was Livia, not the alarm, who woke Montalbano. And it was a beautiful awakening, full of thoughts of life, not death. But as soon as she had left, the clock was back on the bedside table.

✻

'Aah, Chief, Chief!'

'What is it, Cat?'

'There's a lady waiting for you.'

'For me?'

'She din't say what it was f'you poissonally in poisson. She just said she wanted a talk to somebody from the police.'

'So why couldn't she talk to you?'

'Chief, she said she wanted a talk somebody superior to me.'

'Isn't Inspector Augello here?'

'No, sir. He called to say he was comin' in late 'cause he's runnin' late.'

'And why's that?'

'He says last night the baby got sick and so today the medical doctor's gonna come.'

'Cat, you don't have to say "medical doctor", just "doctor" is more than enough.'

'Iss not enough, Chief. Iss confusing. Take you, f'rinstance. You's a doctor but not o' the medical variety.'

'What about the mother — Beba? Can't she wait for the med — the doctor herself?'

'Yessir, Miss Beba's there, Chief, but she says she wants him to be there too.'

'What about Fazio?'

'Fazio's with some kid.'

'What did this kid do?'

'Didn't do nothin, Chief. He's dead.'

'How'd he die?'

'Doverose.'

'OK, tell you what. I'm going into my office now. You wait about ten minutes, then send in the lady.'

The inspector was furious with Augello. Ever since the baby was born, Mimì had hovered over it as much as he'd hovered over women previously. He was head over heels in love with his young son, Salvo. That's right: not only had he called upon the inspector to baptize the kid, he'd also given him the wonderful surprise of naming him after him.

'Can't you give him your father's name, Mimì?'

'Right! Imagine that — my father's called Eusebio.'

'So name him after Beba's father.'

'That'd be even worse. His name's Adelchi.'

'So the real reason you're naming him after me is because all the other available names seem too bizarre to you?'

'Come on, Salvo! First of all, I'm very fond of you, you're like a father to—'

A father? With a son like Mimì?

'Oh, fuck off!'

Livia, upon learning that the newborn would be called Salvo, had burst into tears. Certain special circumstances moved her deeply. 'Mimì loves you so much! Whereas you—'

'Oh, he loves me, does he? Do the names Eusebio and Adelchi mean anything to you?'

And ever since the kid was born, Mimì had appeared at the station and disappeared just as fast: one minute Salvo (junior, of course) had the runs, the next minute he had red spots on his bottom or he was throwing up, the next he didn't want to suckle . . .

He'd complained about it, over the phone, to Livia.

'Oh, yeah? You've got a problem with Mimì? All that means is he's a loving, conscientious father! I'm not so sure that you, in his position—'

He'd hung up on her.

He looked at the morning mail, which Catarella had left on his desk. By prior agreement with the post office, anything addressed to his house in Marinella was being forwarded to the station because sometimes he went a couple of days without returning home. Today there were only official letters, which he set aside, not feeling like reading them. He would hand them over to Fazio as soon as he got back.

The telephone rang.

'Chief, it's Dr Latte wit' an S at the end.'

Lattes, that was, chief of the commissioner's cabinet. To his horror, Montalbano had discovered a while back that Lattes had a clone in a government spokesman who appeared frequently on TV: the same air of the sacristy, the same porky-pink, beardless skin, the same

1

little arselike mouth, the same unctuousness. An exact replica.

'My dear Montalbano, how's it going?'

'Very well, Doctor.'

'And the family? The children? Everything all right?'

He'd told him a million times he neither was married nor had any children, legitimate or illegitimate. But it was hopeless. The man was obsessed. 'Everything's fine.'

'Good, thank the Lord. Listen, Montalbano, the commissioner would like to talk to you at five o'clock this afternoon.'

Why did he want to talk to him? Usually Commissioner Bonetti-Alderighi carefully avoided him, preferring to summon Mimì instead. It must be some colossal pain in the neck.

The door flew open violently, crashed against the wall, and Montalbano jumped out of his chair. Catarella appeared.

'Beck y'pardon, Chief, my 'and slipped. The ten minutes passed just now, just like you said.'

'Oh, yeah? Ten minutes have passed? What the hell do I care?'

'The lady, Chief.'

He'd completely forgotten. 'Is Fazio back?'

'Not yet so far, Chief.'

'Send her in.'

A woman just under forty, who looked, at first glance,

like a former Sister of Mercy: downcast eyes behind her glasses, hair in a bun, hands clenching her bag, the whole wrapped up in a broad grey frock that made it impossible to tell what lay beneath. Her legs, however – despite thick stockings and flat shoes – were long and beautiful. She stood hesitantly in the doorway, staring at the strip of white marble separating the floor tiles of the corridor from those in Montalbano's office.

'Come in, come in. Please close the door and make yourself comfortable.'

She obeyed, sitting on the very edge of one of the two chairs in front of his desk.

'What can I do for you, Signora?'

'Signorina. Michela Pardo. You're Inspector Montalbano, yes?'

'Have we met?'

'No, but I've seen you on television.'

'I'm listening.'

She seemed even more embarrassed. Settling her buttocks more comfortably into the chair, she stared at the toe of one of her shoes, swallowed twice, opened her mouth, closed it, then opened it again. 'It's about my brother, Angelo.'

And she stopped, as though the inspector needed only to know the name of her brother to grasp the whole problem in a flash.

'Signorina Michela, surely you realize—'

'I know, I know. Angelo has ... he's disappeared. It's been two days. I'm sorry, I'm just very worried and confused and—'

'How old is your brother?'

'Forty-two.'

'Does he live with you?'

'No, he lives by himself. I live with Mamma.'

'Is your brother married?'

'No.'

'Does he have a girlfriend?'

'No.'

'What makes you think he's disappeared?'

'Because he never lets a day go by without coming to see Mamma. And when he can't come, he telephones. And if he has to go away, he lets us know. We haven't heard from him for two days.'

'Have you tried calling him?'

'Yes, I've tried his home phone and his mobile. There's no answer. I even went to his house. I rang and rang the doorbell, then decided to go in.'

'You have the key to your brother's place?'

'Yes.'

'And what did you find there?'

'Everything was in perfect order. I was scared.'

'Does your brother suffer from any illness?'

'No.'

'What does he do for a living?'

'He's an informer.'

Montalbano balked. Had ratting on others become an established profession, with a year-end bonus and paid holidays, like Mafia turncoats, who had fixed salaries? He would clear this up in a minute.

'Is he often on the move?'

'Yes, but he works within a limited area. Basically he doesn't go beyond the boundaries of the province.'

'So, do you want to declare him a missing person?'

'No ... I don't know.'

'I should warn you that we can't get moving on it straight away.'

'Why not?'

'Because your brother is an independent adult, healthy in body and mind. He might have decided to go away for a few days of his own accord. Understand? And, in the end, we don't know whether—'

'I understand. What do you suggest I do?'

As she was asking this, she finally looked at him. Montalbano felt a sort of heatwave run through his body. Those eyes were exactly like a deep, violet lake that any man would gladly dive into and drown. It was a good thing Signorina Michela almost always kept them lowered. In his mind, Montalbano took two strokes and swam back to shore.

'Well, I would suggest you go back to your brother's place and have another look.'

'I did, yesterday. I didn't go inside, but I rang the doorbell for a long time.'

'All right – but maybe he's in no condition to come to the door.'

'Why would that be?'

'I dunno. Maybe he slipped in the bath and can't walk, or has a high fever—'

'Inspector, I didn't just ring the doorbell. I called to him. If he'd slipped in the bath, he would have answered. Angelo's apartment isn't very big.'

'I'm afraid I must insist you go back there.'

'I won't go alone. Would you come with me?' She looked at him again.

This time Montalbano found himself sinking, the water coming up to his neck. He thought about it for a moment, then decided. 'Listen, I'll tell you what. If you still haven't heard from your brother by seven o'clock this evening, come back to the station, and I'll accompany you.'

'Thank you.'

She stood up and held out her hand. Montalbano took it but couldn't bring himself to shake it. It felt like a piece of lifeless flesh.

*

Ten minutes later Fazio turned up. 'A seventeen-year-old kid. Went up to the terrace of his building and shot himself up with an overdose. There was nothing we could do, poor guy. When we got there he was already dead. The second in three days.'

Montalbano looked at him, dumbfounded. 'The

second? You mean there was a first? Why wasn't I told about it?'

'Fasulo, the engineer, but with him it was cocaine,' said Fazio.

'Cocaine? What are you saying? Fasulo died of a heart-attack!'

'Well, that's what the death certificate says. It's what his friends say, too. But everybody in town knows it was drugs.'

'Badly cut?'

'That I can't say, Chief.'

'Listen, do you know some guy named Angelo Pardo, forty-two years old and an informer?'

Fazio didn't seem surprised by Angelo Pardo's profession. Maybe he hadn't fully understood. 'No, sir. Why do you ask?'

'Seems he disappeared two days ago and his sister's getting worried.'

'You want me to—'

'No, but later, if there's still no news, we'll see.'

✳

'Inspector Montalbano? This is Lattes.'

'What can I do for you?'

'Family all right?'

'I think we discussed them a couple of hours ago.'

'Of course. Listen, I'm supposed to tell you that the commissioner can't see you today, as you'd requested.'

'Doctor, it was the commissioner who asked to see me.'

'Really? Well, it makes no difference. Could you come tomorrow at eleven?'

'Definitely.'

Upon learning that he wouldn't be seeing the commissioner, his lungs filled with air and he felt suddenly ravenous. Enzo's trattoria was the only solution.

He stepped outside the police station. The day had the colours of summer, without the extreme heat. He walked slowly, taking his time, already tasting what he was about to eat. When he arrived in front of the trattoria, his heart fell to his feet. The restaurant was closed. Locked. What the hell had happened? In rage, he gave the door a swift kick, turned and started to walk away, cursing the saints. He'd taken barely two steps when he heard someone calling him.

'Inspector! Did you forget we're closed today?'

Damn! He had!

'But if you want to eat with me and my wife...'

He dashed back. And ate so much that, as he was eating, he felt embarrassed, ashamed, but couldn't help himself. When he'd finished, Enzo nearly congratulated him. 'To your health, Inspector!'

The walk along the jetty was necessarily a long one. He spent the rest of the afternoon with eyelids drooping and head nodding, overcome by sleepiness. When this happened he would get up and go to wash his face.

At seven o'clock, Catarella told him the lady from the morning had returned.

As soon as she walked in, Michela Pardo said only one word: 'Nothing.'

She did not sit down. She was anxious to get to her brother's place as quickly as possible, and tried to communicate this to the inspector.

'All right,' said Montalbano. 'Let's go.'

Passing Catarella's cubby-hole, he told him: 'I'm going out with the lady. If you need me for anything, I'll be at home later.'

'Will you be coming in my car?' asked Michela Pardo, gesturing towards a blue Polo.

'Perhaps it would be best if I take my own and follow you. Where does your brother live?'

'It's a bit of a way, in the new district. Do you know Vigàta Two?'

He knew Vigàta Two. A nightmare dreamed up by some property speculator under the influence of the worst sort of hallucinogen. He wouldn't live there if he were dead.

2

Luckily for him and the inspector – who never in a million years would have spent more than five minutes in one of those gloomy six-by-ten-foot rooms defined in the brochures as 'spacious and sunny' – Angelo Pardo lived just past the new residential complex of Vigàta Two in a small, restored nineteenth-century villa three storeys high. The front door was locked. As Michela unlocked it, Montalbano noticed that the intercom had six nameplates, which meant there were six apartments, two on the ground floor and four on the other floors.

'Angelo lives on the top floor and there's no lift.'

The staircase was broad and comfortable. The building seemed uninhabited. No voices, no sound of televisions. And yet it was the time of day when people were normally preparing their evening meal.

On the top-floor landing there were two doors. Michela went to the one on the left. Before opening it, she showed the inspector a small window with a grille over it beside the steel-plated door. The little window's shutters were locked.

'I called him from here. Surely he would have heard me.'

She unlocked one, then another lock, turning the key four times, but did not go in. She stepped aside. 'Could you go first?'

Montalbano pushed the door, felt for the light switch, turned it on and entered. He sniffed at the air like a dog. He was immediately convinced that there was no human presence, dead or alive, in the apartment. 'Follow me,' he said to Michela.

The entrance led into a broad corridor. On the left-hand side, a master bedroom, bathroom and another bedroom. On the right, a study, kitchen, small bathroom and a smallish living room. All in perfect order and sparkling clean.

'Does your brother have a cleaning lady?'

'Yes.'

'When did she last come?'

'I couldn't say.'

'Listen, Signorina, do you visit your brother often?'

'Yes.'

'Why?'

The question flustered Michela. 'What do you mean, "why"? He's my brother!'

'Granted, but you said Angelo comes to your and your mother's place practically every other day. So I

17

suppose you come to see him here on the off days? Is that right?'

'Well ... yes. But not so regularly.'

'OK. But why do you need to see each other when your mother's not around?'

'Good God, Inspector, when you put it that way ... It's just something we've been in the habit of doing since we were children ... There's always been, between Angelo and me, a sort of ...'

'Complicity?'

'I suppose you could call it that.' She let out a giggle.

Montalbano decided to change the subject. 'Shall we go and see if a suitcase is missing? If all his clothes are here?'

Michela followed him into the master bedroom. She opened the armoire and looked at all the clothing, one article at a time. Montalbano noticed that it was all expensive, tailored stuff.

'Everything's here. Even the grey suit he was wearing last time he came to see us, three days ago. The only thing missing, I think, is a pair of jeans.'

On top of the armoire, wrapped in cellophane, were two elegant leather suitcases, one large and the other a little smaller.

'The suitcases are here.'

'Does he have an overnight bag?'

'Yes. He usually keeps it in the study.'

They went into the study. The small bag lay beside

the desk. One wall was covered with shelves of the sort one sees in pharmacies, enclosed in sliding glass panels. And in fact the shelves were stocked with a great many medicine containers: boxes, flasks, bottles.

'Didn't you say your brother was an informer?'

'Yes. For the pharmaceutical industry.'

Montalbano understood. Angelo was what used to be called a pharmaceutical representative. But this profession, like dustmen turned 'ecological agents' or cleaning ladies promoted to the rank of 'domestic collaborators' had been ennobled with a new name more appropriate to the elegance of our age. The substance, however, remained the same.

'He used to be – still is, actually – a doctor, but didn't practise for very long,' Michela felt obliged to add.

'Fine. As you can see, Signorina, your brother's not here. If you like, we can go.'

'Let's.' She said it reluctantly, looked all around as if she thought she might, at the last moment, find her brother hiding inside a bottle of pills for liver disease.

Montalbano went ahead, waited for her to turn off the lights and double-lock the door with due diligence. They descended the stairs, silent amid the great silence of the building. Was it empty, or were they all dead? Once outside, Montalbano, seeing how disconsolate she looked, suddenly felt terribly sorry for her. 'You'll hear from your brother soon – you'll see,' he said to her softly, holding out his hand.

But she didn't grasp it, only shook her head still more disconsolately.

'Listen ... your brother ... is he seeing any ... Isn't he in a relationship with anyone?'

'Not that I know of.' She eyed him. And as she did so, Montalbano swam desperately to avoid drowning. All at once the waters of the lake turned very dark, as though night had fallen.

'What's wrong?' he asked.

Without answering, she opened her eyes wide, and the lake turned into open sea.

Swim, Salvo, swim.

'What's wrong?' he repeated, between strokes.

Again she didn't answer. Turning her back to him, she unlocked the door, climbed the stairs, reached the top floor but didn't stop there. The inspector then noticed a recess in the wall with a spiral staircase leading up to a glass door. Michela climbed this and slipped a key into the door, but was unable to open it.

'Let me try,' he said.

He opened the door and found himself on a terrace as big as the villa. Pushing him aside, Michela ran towards a one-room structure, a sort of die standing practically in the middle. It had a door and, to one side, a window. But they were locked.

'I haven't got the key,' said Michela. 'I've never had one.'

'But why do you want...?'

'This used to be the laundry. Angelo rented it with the terrace and transformed it. He comes here sometimes to read or to sun himself.'

'OK, but if you haven't got the key—'

'For heaven's sake, please break down the door.'

'Signorina, I cannot, under any circumstances . . .'

She looked at him. That was enough. With a single shoulder-thrust, Montalbano sent the plywood door flying. He went inside, but before he had even felt for the light switch, he yelled: 'Don't come in!'

He'd detected at once the smell of death in the room.

Michela, however, even in the dark, must have noticed something because Montalbano caught first a stifled sob, then heard her fall to the floor, unconscious.

'What do I do now?' he asked himself, cursing.

He bent down, picked Michela up, and carried her as far as the glass door. Transporting her like that, though – as a groom carries his bride in movies – he would never make it down the spiral staircase. It was too narrow. So he put her down upright, embraced her around the waist, wrapping his hands around her back, and lifted her off the ground. In this way, with care, he could manage it. At moments, he was forced to squeeze her tighter and managed to notice that under the floppy dress, Michela hid a firm, girlish body. At last he arrived in front of the door to the other top-floor apartment and rang the bell, hoping someone was alive in there, or that the sound would at least wake them from the grave.

'Who is it?' asked an angry male voice.

'It's Inspector Montalbano. Could you open the door, please?'

The door opened and King Victor Emmanuel III appeared. An exact replica, that is: the same moustache, the same midget-like stature. Except that he was dressed in civvies. Seeing Montalbano with his arms round Michela, he got entirely the wrong idea and turned bright red.

'Please let me in,' said the inspector.

'What? You want me to let you inside? You're insane! You have the gall to ask me if you can have sex in my home?'

'No, look, Your Majesty, I—'

'Shame on you! I'm going to call the police!' And he slammed the door.

'Fucking idiot!' Montalbano gave the door a swift kick.

Thrown off balance by Michela's weight, he very nearly fell to the floor with her. He picked her up, again like a bride, and started carefully down the stairs. He knocked at the first door he came to.

'Who is it?'

A little boy, aged ten at most.

'I'm a friend of your dad's. Could you open?'

'No.'

'Why not?'

'Because Mamma and Papa told me not to open the door to anyone when they're not in.'

Only then did Montalbano remember that before he had lifted Michela off the ground he'd slipped her handbag over his arm. That was the answer. He carried her back up the stairs, propped her against the wall, holding her upright by pressing his own body against her (in no way unpleasant), opened the bag, took out the keys, opened the door to Angelo's apartment, dragged Michela into the master bedroom, laid her on the bed, went into the bathroom, grabbed a towel, soaked it under the tap, went back into the bedroom, placed the towel over her forehead and collapsed on to the bed, dead tired from the exertion. He was breathing heavily and drenched in sweat.

Now what? He certainly couldn't leave her alone and go back up to the terrace to see how things stood. The problem was immediately resolved.

'There he is!' shouted His Majesty, appearing in the doorway. 'See? He's getting ready to rape her!'

Behind him Fazio, pistol in hand, cursed. 'Please go home, sir.'

'You mean you're not going to arrest him?'

'Go home, now!'

Victor Emmanuel III had another brilliant idea. 'You're an accomplice! An accomplice! I'm going to call the Carabinieri!' He raced out of the room.

Fazio ran after him. He returned five minutes later. 'I managed to convince him. What on earth happened?'

Montalbano told him. Meanwhile he noticed that Michela was regaining consciousness. 'Did you come alone?' he asked.

'No, Gallo's waiting in the car.'

'Get him to come up.'

Fazio called him on his mobile phone, and Gallo arrived in a jiffy.

'Keep an eye on this woman. When she comes round, do not under any circumstance let her go up to the terrace. Got that?'

Followed by Fazio, Montalbano climbed back up the spiral staircase. It was pitch black on the terrace. Night had fallen.

He entered the little room and turned on the light. A table covered with newspapers and magazines. A refrigerator. A sofa-bed for one person. Four long planks affixed to the wall that served as a bookcase. There was a small drinks cabinet with bottles and glasses. A sink in a corner. A large leather armchair of the sort one used to see in offices. He'd set himself up nicely, this Angelo. Who lay collapsed in the armchair, half of his face blasted off by the shot that had killed him. He was dressed in a shirt and jeans – whose zip was open, dick dangling between his legs.

'What should I do – call?' asked Fazio.

'Call,' said Montalbano. 'I'm going downstairs.'

What was he doing there anyway? Soon the whole circus would be there: prosecutor, coroner, crime lab, and Giacovazzo, the new Flying Squad chief, who would lead the investigation. If they needed him, they knew where to find him.

When he went back into the master bedroom, Michela was sitting on the bed, frighteningly pale. Gallo was standing a couple of steps away from her.

'Go up to the terrace and give Fazio a hand. I'll stay here.'

Relieved, Gallo left.

'Is he dead?'

'Yes.'

'How?'

'Gunshot.'

'Oh, my God, oh, my God, oh, my God!' she cried, covering her face with her hands.

But she was a strong woman. She took a sip of water from a glass that Gallo must have given her.

'Why?'

'Why what?'

'Why was he killed? Why?'

Montalbano threw up his hands. But Michela was already beset by another concern. 'Mamma! Oh, my God! How am I ever going to tell her?'

'Don't.'

'But I have to!'

'Listen to me. Telephone her. Tell her we've discovered

that Angelo was in a terrible car accident. That he's in a grave condition. You're going to spend the night at the hospital with him. Don't tell her which one. Does your mother have any relatives around here?'

'Yes, a sister.'

'Does she live in Vigàta?'

'Yes.'

'Call your aunt and tell her the same thing. Ask her to go and stay with your mother. I think it's best if you spend the night here. Tomorrow morning you'll be strong enough to find the right words to tell your mother the truth.'

'Thank you,' said Michela.

She stood up, and Montalbano heard her walk into the study where there was a phone.

He, too, left the bedroom, went into the living room, sat down in an armchair and lit a cigarette.

'Chief? Where are you?'

It was Fazio.

'In here. What is it?'

'I gave the word, Chief. They'll be here in half an hour, max. But Captain Giacovazzo's not coming.'

'Why not?'

'He spoke to the commissioner and the commissioner relieved him. Apparently Giacovazzo's got some delicate matter on his hands. To cut a long story short, the case is yours, like it or not.'

'Fine. Let me know when they get here.'

He heard Michela come out of the study and lock herself into the bathroom between the two bedrooms. Ten minutes later, he heard her come out. She'd washed and put on a woman's dressing-gown. She noticed the inspector was looking at her. 'It's mine,' she explained. 'I used to spend the night here sometimes.'

'Did you talk to your mother?'

'Yes. She took it pretty well, all things considered. And Aunt Iole is already on her way to be with her. You see, Mamma isn't all there in the head. At times she's perfectly lucid, but at others it's as though she's absent. When I told her about Angelo it was as if I was talking about some acquaintance. Perhaps it's for the best. Would you like some coffee?'

'No, thanks. But if you've got a little whisky . . .'

'Of course. I think I'll have some myself.'

She went out, then returned carrying a tray with two glasses and an unopened bottle. 'I'll see if there's any ice.'

'I drink it straight.'

'Me too.'

If a man hadn't been shot dead on the terrace, it might have been the opening scene of an amorous encounter. All that was missing was the background music. Michela heaved a deep sigh, leaned her head against the back of the armchair and closed her eyes. Montalbano decided to lower the boom.

'Your brother was killed either during or after sex. Or while he was masturbating.'

She leaped out of her chair like a fury. 'Imbecile! What are you saying?'

Montalbano behaved as though he hadn't noticed the insult. 'What's so surprising? Your brother was a forty-two-year-old man. You yourself, who used to see him every day, told me he didn't have any women friends. So, let me put the question differently. Did he have any men friends?'

It got worse. She began to tremble, and held out her arm, index finger pointed like a pistol at the inspector.

'You are a – a—'

'Who are you trying to cover for, Michela?'

She fell back into the armchair, weeping, her hands over her face. 'Angelo ... my poor brother ... my poor Angelo ...'

Through the front door, which had been left open, they heard people coming up the stairs.

'I have to go now,' said Montalbano. 'But don't go to bed yet. I'll be back in a little while, so we can continue our conversation.'

'No.'

'Listen, Michela, you can't refuse. Your brother's been murdered and we must—'

'I'm not refusing. I said no to your coming back without notice and asking me more questions when I need to have a shower, take a sleeping pill and go to bed.'

'All right. But I'm warning you, tomorrow will be a hard day for you.'

'Oh, God, oh, God, oh, God! Why?'

One needed the patience of a saint with this woman. 'Michela, were you absolutely certain it was your brother when I broke down the door?'

'Yes,' she said. Huge tears were flowing down her face. She muttered something the inspector didn't understand.

'What did you say?'

'Elena,' she repeated, more clearly.

'Who's she?'

'A woman my brother used to . . .'

'Why did you want to cover up for her?'

'She's married.'

'How long had they been seeing each other?'

'Six months at most.'

'Did they get on well?'

'Angelo told me they quarrelled now and then . . . Elena was . . . is very jealous.'

'Do you know anything about this woman? Her husband's name, where she lives and so on?'

'Yes.'

'Tell me.'

She told him.

'What sort of relationship do you have with Elena Sclafani?'

'I only know her by sight.'

'So you have no reason to tell her what happened to your brother?'

'No.'

'Good. You can go to bed now. I'll pick you up tomorrow morning at around nine thirty.'

3

Somebody must have found the switch for the two lights that lit up the area of the terrace nearest the former laundry room. Judge Tommaseo was walking back and forth in the illuminated area, carefully avoiding the surrounding darkness. Two men in white overalls were sitting on the balustrade with lighted cigarettes in hand. They must have been ambulance workers, waiting for the go-ahead to pick up the body and take it to the morgue.

Fazio and Gallo were standing near the entrance to the room. They'd removed the door from its hinges and propped it against the wall. Montalbano saw Dr Pasquano washing his hands, which meant he'd finished examining the body. The coroner looked angrier than usual. Maybe he'd been interrupted during a game of *briscola* or *tressette*, which he played every Thursday night.

Tommaseo ran up to the inspector. 'What did the sister say?'

Apparently Fazio had told him where Montalbano
was and what he was doing.

'Nothing. I didn't interrogate her.'

'Why not?'

'I wouldn't have dared without you being present,
Dr Tommaseo.'

The public prosecutor puffed out his chest. He
looked like a turkey-cock.

'What were you doing with her all this time?'

'I put her to bed.'

Tommaseo glanced around, then huddled up conspir-
atorially to the inspector. 'Pretty?'

'That's not the right adjective, but I'd say so.'

Tommaseo licked his lips. 'When can I . . . interrogate
her?'

'I'll bring her to your office tomorrow morning,
around ten thirty. Is that OK with you? Unfortunately
I've a meeting with the commissioner at eleven.'

'Fine.' He licked his lips again.

Pasquano came up to them.

'So?' asked Tommaseo.

'So what? Didn't you see him? He was shot in the
face. Once. That was enough.'

'Do you know how long he's been dead?'

Pasquano gave him a dirty look and didn't answer.

'Roughly speaking,' Montalbano bargained.

'What day is today?'

'Thursday.'

'Roughly speaking, I'd say he was shot late Monday evening.'

'Is that all?' Tommaseo cut in again, disappointed.

'I don't think I saw any wounds from assegais or boomerangs,' Pasquano said sarcastically.

'No, no, I was referring to the fact that his member was—'

'Oh, that? You want to know why he had it out? He'd just performed a sexual act.'

'Do you mean he was taken by surprise just after masturbating and killed?'

'I didn't say anything about masturbation,' said Pasquano. 'It might have been oral sex.'

Tommaseo's eyes flashed like a cat's. He lived for such details. Gloried in them. Wallowed in them. 'You think so? The murderess killed him straight after giving him a—'

'What makes you think it was a woman?' asked Pasquano, who, no longer angry, was beginning to amuse himself. 'It could just as easily have been a man.'

'True,' Tommaseo admitted reluctantly. The homo-erotic hypothesis clearly didn't appeal to him.

'Anyway, it's not certain that the victim only had oral sex.'

Pasquano had cast the bait, which the prosecutor swallowed. 'Really?'

'Yes. It's possible that the woman – assuming, for the sake of hypothesis, that it was a woman – was straddling him.'

Tommaseo's eyes turned more catlike than ever.

'Right! And as she was bringing him to orgasm, gazing into his eyes, she already had her hand on the weapon and—'

'Wait a second. What makes you think she looked her victim in the eyes?' Pasquano cut in, a seraphic expression on his face.

Montalbano knew he couldn't take Pasquano's shenanigans for much longer. He'd burst out laughing at any moment.

'But how could she *not* look him in the eyes, in that position?' said Tommaseo.

'We're not certain that that was the position.'

'But you yourself just said—'

'Listen, Tommaseo, the woman might have straddled the man, but we don't know how – that is, whether she was facing him or had her back to him.'

'True.'

'And in the latter case, she wouldn't have been able to look her victim in the eye. Wouldn't you agree? Anyway, from that position, the man would have had an embarrassment of riches. Well, I'm off. Goodnight. I'll keep you informed.'

'Oh, no, you don't! Explain yourself! What do you

mean by "an embarrassment of riches"?' said Tommaseo, running after the coroner.

They disappeared into the darkness.

Montalbano approached Fazio. 'Have Forensics got lost?'

'They'll be here any minute.'

'Listen, I'm going home. You stay here. See you tomorrow at the office.'

He got home in time for the local news. Nobody, of course, knew anything yet about the death of Angelo Pardo, but the two local stations, TeleVigàta and the Free Channel were still talking about another death, and this time the corpse was truly distinguished.

Around eight o'clock on Wednesday, the night before, the honourable Armando Riccobono, a deputy in Parliament, had gone to see his party colleague Senator Stefano Nicotra, who, for the previous five days, had been staying at his country house between Vigàta and Montereale, taking a modest breather from his normally intense political activity. They'd spoken by telephone on Sunday morning and agreed to meet on Wednesday evening.

A seventy-year-old widower with no children, Senator Nicotra, a Vigàta native, was a local and national hero. A former minister of agriculture and twice under-secretary, he he had skilfully navigated all the different currents of the old Christian Democratic party, managing to stay afloat through even the most frightful storms. During the horrific hurricane 'Clean Hands' he had turned into a submarine, navigating under water by means of periscope alone. He resurfaced only when he'd sighted the possibility of casting anchor in a safe port – the one just constructed by the former Milanese property speculator-cum-owner-of-the-top-three-private-nationwide-television-stations-cum-parliamentary-deputy, head of his own personal political party, and finally prime minister. A number of other survivors of the great shipwreck had gone along with Nicotra, and Armando Riccobono was one.

Arriving at the senator's villa, the honourable Riccobono had knocked at the door for a long time to no avail. Alarmed, because he knew the senator was at home alone, he'd walked round the house, looked through a window and seen his friend lying on the floor, either unconscious or dead. Since, given his age, he couldn't very well climb through the window, he had called for help on his mobile phone.

In brief, Senator Nicotra had, as the newspapers liked to put it, 'died of heart failure' on that same Sunday evening after he had spoken to the honourable Riccobono. Nobody'd been to see him on Monday or Tuesday. He himself had told his secretary he wanted to be left alone and undisturbed, and that he was going to unplug his phone. If he needed anything, he would call for it.

TeleVigàta, through the pursed lips of their political commentator Pippo Ragonese, was explaining to one and all the vast sweep of Italy's grief at the loss of the eminent politician. The chief executive – into whose party the senator had fled with his belongings – had sent a message of condolence to the family.

'What family?' Montalbano asked himself.

It was well known that the senator had had no family. And it would have been going too far, indeed it was entirely beyond the realm of possibility, for the chief executive to send a message of condolence to the Sinagra crime family, with whom the senator had apparently had, and continued to have, long and fruitful – but never proven – ties.

Pippo Ragonese concluded by saying that the funeral would be held the following day, Friday, in Montelusa.

Turning off the television, the inspector didn't feel like eating. He decided to sit on the veranda for a while and enjoy the cool sea air, then go to bed.

＊

The alarm went off at seven thirty, and Montalbano shot out of bed like a jack-in-the-box. Shortly before eight, the phone rang.

'Chief, oh, Chief! Doctor Latte wit' an S at the end jes' called!'

'What did he want?'

'He said that 'cause that they're having the furinal service for that sinator that died and seeing as how the c'mishner gotta be there poissonally in poisson, atta

furinal, I mean, the c'mishner can't come to see youse like
he said he was gonna do. Unnastand, Chief?'

'Perfectly, Cat.'

It was a lovely day, but the moment he put down the
receiver it seemed downright heavenly. The prospect of
not having to meet Bonetti-Alderighi made him practically idiotic with joy, to the point at which he composed
a perfectly ignoble couplet — ignoble in terms of intelligence and metre — for the occasion:

> A dead senator a day
> Keeps the commissioner away.

Michela had mentioned that Emilio Sclafani taught
Greek at the *liceo classico* of Montelusa, which probably
meant he got into his car every morning and drove to
school. Thus when the inspector knocked at the door
of Apartment 6, Via Autonomia Siciliana 18, at eight
forty, he was reasonably certain that Signora Elena, the
professor's wife and the late Angelo Pardo's mistress,
would be alone at home. In fact there was no answer.
The inspector tried again. Nothing. He started to worry.
Maybe the woman had asked her husband for a lift and
gone into Montelusa. He knocked a third time. Still
nothing. He turned, cursing, and was about to descend the
stairs when he heard a woman's voice call from inside
the apartment, 'Who is it?'

This question is not always easy to answer. First,
because it may happen that the person who's supposed to

reply is caught at a moment of identity loss and, second, because saying who one is doesn't always facilitate things.

'Administration,' he said.

In so-called civilized societies an administrator is always administrating you, thought Montalbano. It might be the apartments' administrator or a legal administrator, but it makes no difference since what matters is that he's there, and stays there, and that he administrates you more or less carefully, or even secretly, ready to make you pay for mistakes you perhaps don't even know you've made. Joseph K knew a thing or two about this.

The door opened and an attractive, thirtyish blonde appeared in an absurd kimono, with fire-red pouty lips that lacked even a trace of lipstick, and sleepy blue eyes. She'd got out of bed to answer the door and still bore a strong smell of sleep. The inspector felt vaguely uneasy, mostly because, though barefoot, she was taller than him.

'What do you want?'

Her tone made it clear that she had no intention of wasting any time and, indeed, was in a hurry to go back to bed.

'Police. I'm Inspector Montalbano. Good morning. Are you Elena Sclafani?'

She turned pale and took a step backwards. 'Oh, my God, has something happened to my husband?'

Montalbano hadn't been expecting this. 'To your husband? No. Why do you ask?'

'Because every morning, when he gets into his car to

drive to Montelusa, I ... Well, he doesn't know how to drive. Since we got married four years ago he's had about ten minor accidents so—'

'Signora, I didn't come to talk to you about your husband but about another man. And I have many things to ask you. Perhaps we should go inside.'

She took Montalbano into a small but rather elegant living room. 'Please sit down, I'll be back in a moment.'

Ten minutes later, she returned in a blouse and skirt, slightly above the knee, high heels, and with her hair in a bun. She sat down in an armchair in front of the inspector. She showed neither curiosity nor the slightest concern. 'Would you like some coffee?'

'If it's already made ...'

'No, but I'll make some. I need a cup myself. If I don't have coffee first thing in the morning I don't connect.'

'I know exactly what you mean.'

She went into the kitchen and started rummaging around. The telephone rang, and she answered it. She returned with the coffee. They put sugar into their cups, and neither spoke until they'd drained them.

'That was my husband on the phone, calling to let me know he was about to start a class. He does it every day, just to reassure me he got there all right.'

'May I smoke?' Montalbano asked.

'Of course. I do, too ... So,' said Elena, leaning back

in the armchair, a lighted cigarette between her fingers, 'what's Angelo done this time?'

Bewildered, Montalbano gaped at her, his mouth hanging open. For the past half-hour he'd been trying to work out how to broach the subject of the woman's lover, and she had come out with this explicit question. 'How did you know I—'

'Inspector, there are currently two men in my life. You made it clear you hadn't come to talk about my husband, which can only mean you're here about Angelo. Am I right?'

'Yes. But before I go any further, I'd like you to explain that adverb you used. "Currently". What did you mean?'

Elena smiled. She had bright white teeth, like a young wild animal's.

'I mean that at the moment there's Emilio, my husband, and there's Angelo. More often there's only Emilio.'

While Montalbano was contemplating the meaning of this, Elena asked, 'Do you know my husband?'

'No.'

'He's an extraordinary person, good, intelligent, understanding. I'm twenty-nine. He's seventy. He could be my father. I love him. And I try to be faithful to him. I don't always succeed. As you can see, I'm speaking to you with total sincerity, without even knowing the reason for your visit. By the way, who told you about me and Angelo?'

'Michela Pardo.'

'Ah.'

She stubbed out her cigarette in the ashtray and lit another. A wrinkle now furrowed her beautiful brow. She was concentrating very hard. Not only beautiful, she must also be very intelligent. Without warning, two more wrinkles appeared at the corners of her mouth. 'Has something happened to Angelo?'

She'd finally asked.

'He's dead.'

She jolted as though an electrical current had passed through her, and closed her eyes tight. 'Was he murdered?' She was weeping quietly, without sobbing.

'What makes you think there's been a crime?'

'Because if it had been a car accident or a natural death, a police inspector would not have come to interrogate the victim's mistress at eight thirty in the morning.'

Hats off.

'Yes, he was murdered.'

'Last night?'

'We found him yesterday, but he'd been dead since Monday night.'

'How did he die?'

'Shot.'

'Where?'

'In the face.'

She gave a start, and was trembling now as if she was suddenly chilled. 'No, I meant where did it happen?'

'At his place. Do you know that room he had up on the terrace?'

'He showed it to me once.'

'Listen, Signora, I have to ask you some questions.'

'Well, here I am.'

'Did your husband know?'

'About my affair with Angelo? Yes.'

'Was it you who told him?'

'Yes. I never keep anything from him.'

'Was he jealous?'

'Of course, but he can control himself. Anyway, Angelo wasn't the first.'

'Where did the two of you meet?'

'At his place.'

'In the room on the terrace?'

'Never. As I said, he showed it to me once. He told me he went up there to read and sunbathe.'

'How often did you meet?'

'It varied. Normally, when one of us felt like it, we called the other. Sometimes we went as long as four or five days without seeing each other, maybe because I was too busy or because he had to go out on his rounds of the province.'

'Were you ever jealous?'

'Of Angelo? No.'

'But Michela told me you were. And that lately the two of you had been quarrelling.'

'I don't even know Michela. I've never met her. But Angelo used to talk about her. She's mistaken.'

'About what?'

'Our quarrels. Jealousy wasn't the reason.'

'Then what was?'

'I wanted to leave him.'

'You *did*?'

'Why are you so surprised? I didn't feel much for him any more, that's all. And then...'

'And then?'

'And then I realized Emilio was taking it hard, even though he didn't let it show. He hadn't felt so bad before.'

'Angelo didn't want you to leave him?'

'No. I think he was starting to develop feelings for me that he hadn't considered at the start. Where women were concerned, Angelo was rather inexperienced.'

'Forgive my asking, but where were you on Monday evening?'

She smiled. 'I was wondering when you'd ask. I have no alibi.'

'Can you tell me what you did? Did you stay at home? See friends?'

'I went out. Angelo and I had planned to get together on Monday evening at his place around nine o'clock. But

when I went out, I went the wrong way almost unconsciously. And when I realized I kept going, forcing myself
not to turn back. I wanted to see whether I could give
him up when he was waiting to make love to me. I drove
around aimlessly for two hours, then went home.'

'Weren't you puzzled that Angelo didn't contact you
the following morning or in the days that followed?'

'No. I thought he wasn't calling me out of spite.'

'Didn't you try to ring him?'

'No, I would never have done that. It would have
been a mistake. Maybe it really was over between us –
and I felt relieved at the thought of it.'

4

The telephone rang again.

'Excuse me,' said Elena, getting up. But before she left the room, she asked, 'Do you have many more questions? Because I'm sure this is a girlfriend whom I'm supposed to—'

'Ten more minutes at the most.'

Elena went out, answered the phone, returned and sat down. From the way she walked and talked, she seemed completely relaxed. She had already managed to metabolize the news of her lover's death. Maybe it was true that she no longer gave a damn about the man. So much the better. He wouldn't have to hold back.

'There's one thing that now seems a bit ... how shall I put it? ... odd to me. Forgive me, I'm not very good with adjectives ... or maybe it seems odd only to me since I'm – I couldn't...'

He was nonplussed. He didn't know how to put the

question to this beautiful girl, who was a pleasure just to look at.

'Say it,' she encouraged him, with a little smile.

'OK. You told me you went out on Monday evening to go to Angelo's, where he was waiting to make love to you. Is that right?'

'That's right.'

'Were you intending to spend the night with him?'

'No. I never spent the night there. I would have come home around midnight.'

'So you would have been with Angelo for about three hours.'

'More or less. But why?'

'Did you ever happen to arrive late for a date with him?'

'A few times.'

'And how did he behave?'

'How was he supposed to behave? He was usually nervous, irritated, but would calm down slowly and...' Her smile now was entirely different from before. Half concealed, secret, self-directed, the eyes sparkling with amusement. '... and try to make up for lost time.'

'What if I were to tell you that Angelo didn't wait for you that evening?'

'What do you mean? I don't think he went out – you said they found him on the terrace.'

'He was killed just after he'd had sex.'

She was either as great an actress as La Duse or truly

shaken. She made a few meaningless gestures, stood up, sat down, brought her empty coffee cup to her lips, put it down, pulled a cigarette out of her packet but didn't light it, stood up, sat down and knocked over a small wooden box on the coffee-table.

'That's absurd,' she said finally.

'You see, Angelo behaved as if he was sure you wouldn't be at his place on Monday evening. Out of resentment towards you, or spite, or to get back at you, he may have called another woman. And now you must answer me truthfully. That evening, as you were driving around in your car, did you phone him and tell him you weren't going to his place?'

'No. That's why it's absurd. Once, you know, I was two hours late and he was beside himself, but still waiting. On Monday evening he had no way of knowing what I'd decided. I could have descended on him at any moment and surprised him.'

'I don't think so,' said Montalbano.

'Why?'

'Because Angelo had taken precautions. He'd gone up to the room on the terrace, and the glass door leading to it was locked. Do you have a key to that door?'

'No.'

'So even if you'd arrived unexpectedly, there was no way you could have surprised him. Do you have keys to his apartment?'

'No.'

'All you could have done was knock on the apartment door, and nobody would have answered. Before long you would have concluded that Angelo wasn't at home, that he'd gone out, perhaps to blow off steam, and you'd have given up. In his room on the terrace, Angelo was out of your reach.'

'But not the killer's,' Elena said, almost angrily.

'That's another matter,' said Montalbano. 'And you can be of help to me in this.'

'How?'

'How long had you been with Angelo?'

'Six months.'

'During that time did you meet any of his friends, male or female?'

'Inspector, perhaps I didn't make myself clear. Our encounters were ... let's say they were very precise in their purpose. I would go to his place, we'd have a whisky, get undressed and go to bed. We never went to the cinema together or to a restaurant. More recently he'd wanted to do that sort of thing, but I didn't. And that also led to quarrels.'

'Why didn't you want to go out with him?'

'Because I didn't want people to laugh at Emilio.'

'But surely Angelo must have spoken to you about some of his friends or girlfriends.'

'He did. Shortly after we met, he told me he'd just broken up with a girl called Paola – "the Red", as he called her. He also told me about a certain Martino, with whom he often had lunch and dinner. But the person he talked about most was his sister Michela. They were very close, and had been since childhood.'

'What do you know about Paola?'

'I've already told you everything I know: Paola, red hair.'

'Did he talk about his job?'

'No. Once he said it paid well, but was boring.'

'Did you know he'd had a medical practice for a while, then gave it up?'

'Yes. But he didn't give it up. The only time he ever spoke to me about it he said some episode had forced him to stop practising. I didn't probe because I didn't care.'

This was new. He had to find out more. Montalbano stood up. 'Thank you for being so open with me. It's a rare thing, I assure you. I think, though, that I'll need to talk to you again.'

'Whatever you say, Inspector. But, please, will you do me a favour?'

'At your service.'

'Next time don't come so early in the morning. The afternoon would be fine. As I said, my husband knows everything. Sorry — it's just that I'm a late riser.'

*

He pulled up in front of Angelo Pardo's building more than half an hour late. But he could take his time because the meeting with the commissioner had been postponed. He pressed the intercom, and Michela buzzed open the door. As he was climbing the stairs, the building still seemed dead. No voices, no other sounds. Had Elena, when she was coming to see Angelo, ever run into any of the other tenants?

Michela was waiting for him at the door. 'You're late.'

Montalbano noticed she was wearing a different dress, but it, too, had been made to hide what could not be hidden. She'd also changed her shoes.

Did she keep a whole wardrobe in her brother's apartment?

Michela understood what was going through the inspector's head. 'I went home early this morning. I wanted to see how Mamma was and took the opportunity to change.'

'This morning you have to see Public Prosecutor Tommaseo. I'd meant to go with you, but there's no point in my being there.'

'What does he want from me?'

'He needs to ask you some questions about your brother. Could I use the telephone? I'll tell him you're on your way.'

'Where do I go?'

'To the courthouse in Montelusa.'

He went into the study and immediately sensed that something had changed, but he didn't know what. He called Tommaseo and told him he couldn't attend the meeting with Pardo's sister.

In the hallway, Michela was ready to leave.

'Could you please give me the keys to this apartment?'

She hesitated, unsure, then opened her bag and handed him the set. 'What if I need to get in?'

'Come to the station and I'll give them back to you. Where can I find you this afternoon?'

'At home.'

He closed the door behind her and ran into the study.

From time immemorial the inspector had had a photo-graphic memory. When, for example, he entered a room that was new to him, he could capture in a single glance not only the arrangement of the furniture but also the objects on top of the various pieces. And he would remember all this even after some time had passed.

He stopped in the doorway, leaned his right shoulder against the jamb and, looking very carefully, saw at once what didn't tally.

The overnight bag.

The previous evening it had been upright on the floor beside the desk. Now it was under the desk. There had been no reason to move it: it was not in the way, even if one had to use the phone. Michela must have picked it up to see what was inside and not put it back where it had been.

He cursed. Shit. He'd made a big mistake. He shouldn't have left the woman alone in the murdered man's home. He had made it as easy as possible for her to get rid of anything that might prove compromising for her brother.

He grabbed the overnight bag and put it on the desk. The little suitcase opened at once; it wasn't locked. Inside, he found a mass of papers with the letterheads of several pharmaceutical companies, instructions for medicines, order forms, receipts.

There were also two diaries, one large and one small. He looked first at the big one. The index of addresses was densely packed with the names and telephone numbers of doctors across the province, hospitals and pharmacies. In addition, Angelo Pardo had diligently written down every work-related appointment he'd had.

Montalbano set this aside and thumbed through the smaller one, Pardo's private diary. It contained the names and phone numbers of Elena Sclafani, his sister Michela, and many others the inspector didn't recognize. He looked at the page for the previous Monday. Pardo had written: '9 pm E.' So, what Elena had told him about her rendezvous with Angelo had been true. He set aside the small diary too, and picked up the phone. 'Montalbano here, Cat. Let me talk to Fazio.'

'OK, Chief.'

'Fazio, could you come over and meet me straight away at Angelo Pardo's place?'

'Are you on the terrace?'

'No, downstairs in the apartment.'

'I'm on my way.'

'Oh, and bring Catarella with you.'

'*Catarella?*'

'Why? Can't he be moved?'

The desk had three drawers. He opened the one on the right. Here, too, papers and documents relating to the man's career as — what was it again? Ah, yes, as a 'pharmaceutical industry informer'. The one in the middle wouldn't open. It was locked and the key was nowhere to be seen. Probably Michela had taken it. What a stupid fuck he'd been! He was about to open the drawer on the left when the telephone on the desk rang so suddenly and loudly that it startled him. He picked up the receiver.

'Yes?' he said, squeezing his nostrils with the index finger and thumb of his right hand to alter his voice.

'You got a cold?'

'Yes.'

'Izzat why you din't come lass night, scumbag? I'll be waitin f'r ya t'night. And ya better come, even if you got pneumonia.'

End of phone call. A man of few but dangerous words. A commanding voice. Surely some doctor upset at a pharmaceutical informer's failure to turn up would not call him a scumbag. Montalbano picked up the big diary and looked at the page for the previous day, Thursday. The part for the evening was blank, but the morning featured an engagement in Fanara with a Dr Caruana.

He was about to open the left-hand drawer when the phone rang again. Montalbano began to suspect there was some connection between the drawer and the telephone. 'Yes?' he said, doing the same rigmarole with his nostrils.

'Dr Angelo Pardo?'

The voice of a woman, fiftyish and stern.

'Yes.'

'Your voice sounds strange.'

'A cold.'

'Ah. I'm a nurse with Dr Caruana in Fanara. The doctor waited a long time for you yesterday morning, and you didn't even have the courtesy to inform us you weren't coming.'

'Please give my apologies to Dr Caruana, but this cold ... I'll get in tou—' He interrupted himself. Wasn't he taking this a bit too far? How could the dead man he was pretending to be ever get in touch?

'Hello?' said the nurse.

'I'll call back as soon as I can. Goodbye.'

He hung up. An entirely different tone from that used by the unknown man in the first phone call. Very interesting. But would he ever succeed in opening the drawer? He moved his hand carefully, keeping it out of the telephone's view.

This time he succeeded.

ANDREA CAMILLERI

It was stuffed full of papers. Every imaginable receipt
of the sort that keep a household running: rent, elec-
tricity, gas, telephone, maintenance. But nothing concerning Angelo, personally in person, as Catarella would say.
Maybe he'd kept the papers more directly related to his
life in the middle drawer.

He closed the left-hand drawer and the telephone
rang. Perhaps it had realized a bit late that he'd tricked
it, and was now taking revenge.

'Yes?' Again with nostrils plugged.

'What the hell happened to you, asshole?'

Male voice, fortyish, angry. He was about to respond
when the other continued: 'Hold on a second, I've got a
call on the other line.'

Montalbano's ears pricked, but he could hear only a
confused murmur. Then two words loud and clear.
'Fuck's sake!'

Then the other hung up. What did it mean? Scumbag
and asshole. It was anyone's guess as to how a third
anonymous caller might define Angelo. At that moment
the intercom sounded. The inspector went and buzzed
open the door downstairs. It was Fazio and Catarella.

'Aah, Chief, Chief! Fazio tol' me you was needin' me
poissonally in poisson!'

He was all sweaty and excited by the high honour the
inspector was bestowing on him in asking him to take
part in the investigation.

'Follow me, both of you.' He led them into the study.

'You, Cat, take the laptop that's on the desk and see if you can tell me everything it's got inside it. But don't do it in here. Take it into the living room.'

'Can I also take the prinner wit' me, Chief?'

'Take whatever you need.'

With Catarella gone, Montalbano filled Fazio in on everything, from his fuck-up in leaving Michela alone in Angelo's apartment to what Elena Sclafani had told him. He also told him about the phone calls. Fazio stood there pensively. 'Tell me again about the second call,' he said, after a moment.

Montalbano described it again.

'Here's my hypothesis,' said Fazio. 'Let's say the guy who phoned the second time is called Giacomo. This Giacomo doesn't know that Angelo's been killed. He calls him and hears him answer the phone. Giacomo's angry because he's been unable to get in touch with Angelo for several days. When he's about to start talking to him, he tells him to hold on because he's got a call on another line. Right?'

'Right.'

'He talks on the other line and somebody tells him something that not only upsets him but makes him break off the conversation. The question is, what did they tell him?'

'That Angelo's been murdered,' said Montalbano.

'That's what I think, too.'

'Listen, Fazio, do the press know about the murder yet?'

'Well, something's leaked out. But to get back to our discussion, when Giacomo finds out he's talking to a fake Angelo, he hangs up immediately.'

'And why *did* he hang up?' said Montalbano. 'Here's a first idea. Let's say Giacomo's a man with nothing to hide, an innocent friend from nights of wining, dining and girls. While he's thinking he's talking to Angelo, somebody tells him Angelo's been killed. A real friend wouldn't have hung up. He'd have asked the fake Angelo who he really is and why he was passing himself off as Angelo. So, we need a second idea. Which is that Giacomo, as soon as he learns of Angelo's death, says, "Fuck's sake," and hangs up because he's afraid of giving himself away if he keeps on talking. So it's not an innocent friendship but something shady. And that first phone call seemed fishy to me too.'

'What can we do?'

'We can try to find out where the calls came from. See if you can get authorization, then take it to the phone company. There's no guarantee it'll work, but it's worth a try.'

'I'll get on to it now.'

'Wait, that's not all. We need to find out everything we can about Angelo Pardo. Based on what Elena Sclafani told me, it seems he was struck off the register of the

Medical Association or whatever it's called. And that's not the sort of thing that's done for chickenshit.'

'I'll see what I can do.'

'Wait. What's the hurry? I also want to know the whole life story of Emilio Sclafani, who teaches Greek at the Montelusa *liceo*. You'll find the address in the phone book.'

'All right,' said Fazio, making no more sign of leaving.

'Another thing. What about Angelo's wallet?'

'He had it in the back pocket of his jeans. Forensics grabbed it.'

'Did they grab anything else?'

'Yes, sir. A set of keys and the mobile phone that was on the table.'

'Before the day is over I want those keys, the phone and the wallet.'

'Fine. Can I go now?'

'No. Try to open the middle drawer of Pardo's desk. It's locked. But you have to do it so it looks like it hasn't been touched.'

'That'll take time.'

'And you've got all the time you need.'

As Fazio started to fiddle with the drawer, Montalbano went into the living room. Catarella had turned on the laptop and was fiddling around himself.

'Iss rilly difficult, Chief.'

'Why?'

''Cause iss got the last word.'

Montalbano was befuddled. What? Can computers talk now? 'Cat, what the hell are you saying?'

'Iss like diss, Chief. When summon don't want summon to look at the poissonal tings he got inside, he gives it a lass word.'

Montalbano understood. 'You mean a password?'

'Ain't dat what I said? And if you don't got the lass word, y'can't get in.'

'So we're fucked?'

'Not nicissarily, Chief. He's gotta have a form wit' the name 'n' sirname o' the owner, date a boith, name o' the missus or girlfriend or brother and sister and mother and father, son if you got one, daughter if you got one—'

'All right, I'll have everything to you today after lunch. Meanwhile take the computer back to the station with you. Who are you going to give the form to?'

'Who'm I sposta give it to, Chief?'

'Cat, you said, "He's gotta have." Who's "he"?'

'He's me, Chief.'

Fazio called him from the study.

5

'I got lucky, Chief. I found a key of my own that seemed like it was made for that lock. Nobody'll be able to tell it's been opened.'

The drawer looked to be in perfect order.

A passport, whose details Montalbano wrote down for Catarella; contracts stating percentages to be earned on products sold; two legal documents from which Montalbano copied down, again for Catarella's benefit, the names and birthdates of Michela and her mother, whose first name was Assunta; a medical defence, folded in four, dating from sixteen years ago; a letter from the Medical Association, dated ten years earlier, informing Angelo that he had been struck off, without any explanation as to why; an envelope with a thousand euros in fifties; two mini-albums with photos from a trip to India and another to Russia; three letters from Signora Assunta to her son, in which she complained about her life with Michela and other similar matters, all personal, but all, well, utterly useless to Montalbano. There was even an old declaration concerning the recovery, in the mother's apartment, of a pistol formerly belonging to Pardo's father. But there was no trace of the weapon. Perhaps Angelo had got rid of it.

'But didn't this gentleman have a bank account?' asked Fazio. 'How is it there are no chequebooks anywhere, not even stubs, or bank statements?'

No answer was forthcoming, since Montalbano was wondering the same thing.

One thing, however, that puzzled the inspector more than a little, and stumped Fazio too, was the discovery of a small dog-eared booklet entitled *The Most Beautiful Italian Songs of All Time*. Though there was a television in the living room, there was no sign anywhere of records, CDs, a CD-player or even a radio.

'How about the room on the terrace? Did you see any discs, headphones or a stereo there?'

'Nothing, Chief.'

So why would somebody keep a booklet of song lyrics locked in a drawer? Most striking was that the book looked as if it had been often consulted: two detached pages had been carefully stuck back in place with Sellotape. Moreover, numbers had been written in the narrow margins. Montalbano studied these, and it didn't take him long to realize that Angelo had jotted down the metre of the lines.

'You can close it now. By the way, did you say you found a set of keys in the room upstairs?'

'Yeah. Forensics took it.'

'I repeat, I want that wallet, phone and the keys this afternoon. What are you doing?'

Instead of closing and locking the drawer, Fazio was emptying on to the desk, in orderly fashion, all the things inside it.

'Just a second, Chief. I want to look at something.'

When the drawer was empty, Fazio pulled it out from its runners and turned it over. Underneath, on the bottom, was a chrome-plated, squat, notched key, stuck to the wood with two pieces of Sellotape.

'Well done, Fazio.'

While the inspector was contemplating the key he'd detached, Fazio put everything back in the drawer in the same order as before, and locked it with his own key, which he slipped back into his pocket.

'If you ask me, this key opens up a wall-safe,' the inspector surmised.

'If you ask me, too,' said Fazio.

'And you know what that means?'

'It means we need to get down to work,' said Fazio, taking off his jacket and rolling up his sleeves.

✻

After two hours spent moving paintings, mirrors, furniture, rugs, medicines and books, Montalbano's pithy conclusion was: 'There's not a bloody thing here.'

They sat down, exhausted, on the living-room sofa.

They looked at one another. And thought the same thing: 'The room upstairs.'

They climbed the spiral staircase. Montalbano opened the glass door, and they were on the terrace. The door to the little room had not been put back on its hinges, but was leaning in place with a piece of paper taped to it forbidding entry because this was a crime scene. Fazio moved the door aside, and they went in.

They had two strokes of luck. First, the room was small so they didn't have to break their backs shifting too much furniture. Second, the table had no drawers, so they didn't waste much time. But the result was the same as it had been in the apartment downstairs, which the inspector had brilliantly, though perhaps not so elegantly, summed up in few words. The one difference was that they were sweating profusely since the sun was beating down on the little room.

'Maybe the key is for a safe-deposit box at a bank,' ventured Fazio, when they had returned to the apartment.

'I doubt it. Usually those keys have a number on them, or an imprint, something to enable bank staff to recognize it. This one is smooth, anonymous.'

'So, what are we going to do?'

'We're going to go and eat,' said Montalbano, waxing poetic.

*

After a thorough bellyful and a slow, meditative-digestive stroll, one step at a time, to the lighthouse and back, Montalbano went to the office.

'Chief, djou bring me the form that he needs?' asked Catarella, the moment he walked in.

'Yes, give it to him.'

According to the complex Catarellian language, 'him' referred to Catarella himself.

The inspector sat down, pulled out the key Fazio had found, laid it on the desk and stared at it as though he wanted to hypnotize it. But the opposite thing happened. The key hypnotized him. In fact, a few minutes later, he let his eyes shut, overwhelmed by an irresistible desire to sleep. He got up, went to wash his face – and had a brainwave. He called Galluzzo in.

'Do you know where Orazio Genco lives?'

'The thief? Of course I do. I went there twice to arrest him.'

'I want you to go and see him, ask him how he's getting on, and give him my regards. Did you know he hasn't got out of bed for a year? I don't feel up to seeing what kind of state he's in.'

Galluzzo wasn't surprised. He knew the inspector and the old burglar were fond of each other and, in their own way, had become friends. 'Anything else?'

'Yes. While you're at at it, let him have a look at this key.' Montalbano took it out and handed it to him.

'Make him tell you what kind it is, and what he thinks it's for.'

'Bah!' said a sceptical Galluzzo. 'It's a modern one.'

'So?'

'Orazio's old, and hasn't worked for years.'

'Don't worry, he keeps himself informed.'

✲

As Montalbano was drifting off to sleep again, Fazio appeared with a plastic bag in his hand.

'Have you been shopping?'

'No, Chief, I went to Montelusa to get what you wanted from Forensics. It's all in here.' He put the bag on the desk. 'And I talked to the phone company. I got the authorization. They're going to try to identify the phones those calls came from.'

'And the information on Angelo Pardo and Emilio Sclafani?'

'Chief, unfortunately I'm not God. I can only do one thing at a time. I'm going out to do the rounds now, see what I can find out. Oh, one more thing. Three.' And he held up the thumb, index and middle finger of his right hand.

Befuddled, Montalbano stared at him. 'Have you become a Freemason recently? Or do you want to play stone, paper, scissors?'

'Chief, you remember the kid who died from an overdose? And that I told you Engineer Fasulo was also killed by drugs, even though everybody said it was a heart-attack?'

'Of course. Who's the third?'

'Senator Nicotra.'

Montalbano's mouth took the shape of an O. 'Is that a joke?'

'No, Chief. It was well known that the senator messed around with drugs. Every now and then he'd shut himself up in his villa and take a three-day trip. Looks like this time he forgot to buy a return ticket.'

'Can this really be true?'

'Gospel, Chief.'

'But Nicotra was forever preaching morality! Tell me something, when you went to the kid's house did you find the usual stuff – syringe, rubber hose?'

'Yes.'

'With Nicotra it must have been something else, some badly cut stuff. I just don't get it. I don't understand these things. Anyway, may he rest in peace.'

Fazio turned to leave and almost collided with Mimì Augello in the doorway.

'Mimì! What a lovely surprise! A sight for sore eyes!'

'Leave me alone, Salvo, I haven't slept a wink for two days.'

'Is the little one ill?'

'He cries all the time for no reason.'

'That's your opinion.'

'But the doctors—'

'Forget about the doctors. Obviously the child's annoyed with you and Beba for bringing him into the world. And, with the way the world is, I can't say I blame him.'

'Don't start. I just wanted to let you know that five minutes ago I had a call from the commissioner.'

'So? Nowadays you and Bonetti-Alderighi are hand-in-glove with each other — except it's not clear who's the hand and who's the glove.'

'Have you finished? Can I talk now? Yes? The commissioner told me that tomorrow morning, around eleven, Inspector Liguori's coming here, to the station.'

Montalbano darkened. 'The idiot from Narcotics?'

'The idiot from Narcotics.'

'What does he want?'

'I don't know.'

'I don't even want to see his shadow.'

'That's precisely why I came in to tell you. Tomorrow, as of eleven o'clock, you should make yourself scarce. I'll talk to him.'

'Thanks. My best to Beba.'

He phoned Michela Pardo. He wanted to see her, not only to ask her some questions but also to find out what she'd taken out of her brother's apartment and why. The stupidity of having let her sleep at Angelo's place weighed heavily on his mind.

'How did it go this morning with Judge Tommaseo?' he asked.

'He made me wait for half an hour in the anteroom, then sent someone to inform me that the meeting had been postponed until the same time tomorrow. I'm glad you rang, Inspector. I was about to call you.'

'What is it?'

'I wanted to know when we could have Angelo back. For the funeral.'

'To be honest, I don't know. But I'll find out. Listen, could you pop into the station?'

'Inspector Montalbano, I decided it was best to tell Mamma that Angelo is dead. I said he'd died in a car accident. She lost control of herself and I had to call our doctor. He gave her some sedatives, and she's resting now. I don't want to leave her alone. Couldn't you come here?'

'Of course. When?'

'Whenever you like. I can't leave the house.'

'I'll be with you around seven this evening. What's your address?'

About an hour later, Galluzzo returned.

'How's Orazio?'

'Pretty far gone, Chief. He wants you to go and see him.' He pulled the key out of his pocket and handed it to the inspector. 'According to Orazio, this is the key to a portable Exeter strongbox, around eighteen inches by twelve and ten inches tall. He says you couldn't open one with an anti-tank mine. You've got to have the key.'

He and Fazio had searched the apartment and the

room on the terrace for a wall safe. Surely they would have seen a strongbox of that size. Which must mean that somebody had taken it away. But what use was it without the key? Or maybe the person who took it had a duplicate. And did Michela know anything about this? It was becoming more and more necessary to talk to her. He'd promised her he would find out about the funeral so he telephoned Pasquano. 'Hello, Doctor, am I disturbing you?'

You had to approach Pasquano carefully. He had a decidedly nasty, unstable character.

'Of course you're disturbing me. Actually, to be precise, you're breaking my balls. You've made me get blood all over the receiver.'

Someone else who didn't know the doctor would have apologized profusely and hung up. But the inspector had been associated with him for so long that he knew it was better sometimes to throw fuel on the fire.

'Doctor, I don't give a fuck.'

'About what?'

'Whether I'm disturbing you or not.'

It worked. Pasquano let out a belly laugh. 'What do you want?'

'Angelo Pardo's family would like to know when they can have the body for the funeral.'

'Five.'

What the hell was getting into Fazio and the doctor?

Had they become Cumaean sibyls? Why had they taken to reciting numbers?

'What does that mean?'

'I'll tell you what it means. It means that before I get to Pardo, I have five other autopsies to perform. Therefore the family will have to wait. Tell them their dear departed is not having such a bad time of it in the freezer. Oh, and while I've got you on the line, I should tell you I was mistaken.'

Madunnuzza santa! The patience one needed with this man!

'About what, Doctor?'

'About whether Pardo had had sex before he was killed. I'm sorry to disappoint Judge Tommaseo, who was off to such a flying start.'

'So you did examine him?'

'Superficially, and only the part I was curious about.'

'But, then, why . . . ?'

'Why was it out, you mean?'

'Exactly.'

'Well, maybe he'd gone for a piss in a corner of the terrace and didn't have time to put it away. Or perhaps he was planning a moment of solitary pleasure but they beat him to it and shot him. But that sort of thing's not my province. It's you, Inspector, who's conducting the investigation, isn't it?'

He hung up without saying goodbye.

So, come to think of it, Elena had been right when she'd refused to believe that Angelo had entertained another woman while he was waiting for her. But the doctor's hypothesis didn't hold water either.

There was no bathroom in the former laundry room, just a sink. If Angelo had needed to go and not felt like running down to his flat, he could have used the sink.

And the masturbation hypothesis wasn't convincing either.

Yet it was odd that Pardo hadn't had time to do up his trousers. No, there must be some other explanation. Something not as simple as Pasquano's theories.

Mimì Augello appeared in the doorway.

'What?'

He had dark circles under his eyes, worse than when he used to spend his nights womanizing.

'Seven,' said Mimì.

Suddenly Montalbano appeared to go mad. He sprang out of his chair, red in the face, and screamed so loudly they must have heard him all the way to the port: 'Eighteen, twenty-four, thirty-six! Fuck! And seventy, too!'

Chaos erupted all over the station, doors slamming, footsteps racing. In an instant Galluzzo, Gallo and Catarella were in the doorway.

'What's going on?'

'What happened?'

'What's up?'

'Nothing, nothing,' said Montalbano, sitting back

down. 'Go back to whatever you were doing. I had a little attack of nerves, that's all. It's over.'

Galuzzo, Gallo and Catarella left, but Mimì was still staring at him. 'What got into you? What were those mysterious numbers about?'

'Ah, so it's me who's being mysterious with numbers. Didn't you come in here and say, "Seven"?'

'Is that a mortal sin now?'

'Never mind. What did you want to tell me?'

'That since Liguori's coming tomorrow I did some research. You know how many drugs deaths we've had in the province in the last ten days?'

'Seven,' said Montalbano.

'Exactly. How did you know?'

'Mimì, you told me yourself. Let's drop the Campanile dialogue.'

'What campanile?'

'Forget it, or I'll have another attack.'

'Do you know what people are saying about Senator Nicotra?'

'That he died of the same illness as the other six.'

'And that explains why Montelusa Narcotics has decided to move in. Haven't you had any ideas?'

'No, and I don't want to.'

Mimì left and the phone rang. 'Inspector Montalbano? Lattes here. Everything all right?'

'Just fine, Doctor, with the Virgin's good grace.'

'The pups?'

What the fuck was he talking about? The children? How many did he think he had? What do puppies do, anyway?

'They're growing, Doctor.'

'Good, good. I wanted to let you know that the commissioner will expect you tomorrow afternoon between five and six.'

'I'll definitely be there.'

It was time to go and see Michela.

As he went past Catarella's cubby-hole, he saw him with his head buried in Angelo Pardo's laptop. 'Getting anywhere, Cat?'

Catarella started and leaped to his feet.

'Aaah, Chief, Chief! We's sinkin' fast! The last word's got the last word! I can't get in! Iss impetrinable!'

'You can't do it?'

'Chief, even if I gotta stay up and awake all night, I'm gonna find that first secret word!'

'Cat, why did you say "first"?'

''Cause, Chief, there's tree files that got past words.'

'Let me get this straight. If it takes you ten hours to find the password to one file, it'll take you at least thirty to find all three?'

'Just like you say, Chief.'

'Best of luck. And if you find the first, don't hesitate to ring me, no matter the time.'

6

He got into the car and set off, but after he'd gone a hundred yards he slapped his forehead, cursed and began a dangerous U-turn. The three motorists behind him let him know vociferously that: one, he was a tremendous *cornuto*; two, his mother was a woman of easy virtue; three, his sister was worse than his mother.

Back at the station, he walked past Catarella without the other noticing, engrossed as he was in the laptop. A whole regiment of gangsters could have entered those offices without a single shot being fired.

In his room, he opened the bag Fazio had brought him and pulled out Angelo's keys. He immediately noticed a key that looked exactly like the one he had in his pocket, which was supposed to open a strongbox. Normally those locks came equipped with only two keys. The one they'd found under the drawer must be the spare.

So he'd been wrong about Michela. She couldn't have taken the strongbox: she had no way to open it.

Perhaps it hadn't disappeared from Angelo's apartment because it had never been there in the first place. Perhaps he kept it elsewhere.

Where elsewhere?

He slapped his forehead again. He was conducting this investigation like a senile old fool who forgot the most basic things. Angelo was a pharmaceutical representative and travelled all over the province, didn't he? Why hadn't it already occurred to him that Angelo must have a car and also, perhaps, a garage?

He emptied Fazio's bag on to the table. Mobile phone. Wallet. And car keys. QED: he *was* a senile old fool.

He put everything back into the bag and took it with him. Catarella didn't notice him this time either.

*

Michela was wearing a loose, shapeless dressing-gown, which a large, slack knot turned into a kind of prison-overall, and a pair of slippers. She kept her dangerous eyes lowered. What sins or evil intentions was her body guilty of for her to punish it by hiding it in that way?

She led him into the living room. Finely crafted old furniture, certainly heirlooms handed down from father to son.

'Forgive me for receiving you in these clothes, but since I'm constantly having to look after Mamma...'

'Not at all. How is she?'

'Luckily she's asleep at the moment. It's the sedatives. The doctor says it's best this way. But it's as if she's having nightmares – she tosses and turns, moaning all the time.'

'I'm sorry,' said Montalbano, who never knew what to say in such circumstances and therefore stuck to generalities.

She broached the question. Directly. 'Did you find anything at Angelo's apartment?'

'What do you mean by "anything"?'

'Anything that might help you to understand who—'

'Nothing yet.'

'You made me a promise.'

Immediately Montalbano understood.

'I phoned Montelusa. They're going to need at least three more days before they can return the body. But don't worry, I'll keep you informed.'

'Thanks.'

'You asked if we'd found anything in your brother's apartment and I said no. But we haven't found either what should be there.'

He'd cast the baited hook. But she didn't bite. She just looked a bit shocked, which was understandable. 'Such as?' she asked.

'Did your brother earn a good living?'

'Good enough. But don't get the wrong idea, Inspector. Perhaps it's better to say he made enough for his needs and ours.'

'Where did he keep his money?'

Michela seemed surprised by the question. 'In the bank.'

'Then how can you explain that we haven't found any chequebook or bank statements?'

Unexpectedly Michela smiled. 'I'll be back in a minute,' she said.

She reappeared with a big portfolio, which she put on the coffee-table. She opened it and pulled out a chequebook for the Banca dell'Isola, searched a bit more, pulled out a sheet of paper and handed both items to the inspector. 'Angelo has an account with this bank, and that's the most recent statement.'

Montalbano looked at the figure in the credit column: ninety-one thousand euros. He handed it, with the chequebook, to Michela, who put them back into the portfolio.

'That money's not all Angelo's. About fifty thousand euros of it are mine, an inheritance left me by an uncle who was particularly fond of me. As you can see, my brother and I pooled our resources. In fact, the bank account is in both our names.'

'How is it that you have the books?'

'Well, Angelo was often out of town on business trips and had trouble meeting certain deadlines. So I paid the bills and gave him the receipts. Did you find them?'

'Yes. Did he have a garage as well as the apartment and the terrace?'

'Of course. There are three garages behind the building. His is the first on the left.'

See, dear Montalbano, you *are* getting senile!

'Why do you say that Angelo couldn't make his payments on time because he was out of town? Weren't most of his trips rather brief and limited to this province?'

'Not entirely. He used to go abroad at least once every three months.'

'Where to?'

'I don't know – Germany, Switzerland, France … The countries where the big pharmaceutical firms are located. They would summon him.'

'I see. Would he stay away long?'

'It varied. From three days to a week, no more.'

'Among your brother's keys we found one that was rather unusual.' He took it out of his pocket and handed it to her. 'Do you recognize it?'

She looked curiously.

'No, but I must have seen one rather like it among his other keys.'

'Did you never ask him what it was for?'

'No.'

'It opens a portable strongbox.'

'Really?' She looked at him.

Bright, inviting eyes, to all appearances. In no way perilous. But be careful, Montalbano. Underneath, hidden, there are probably tangles of giant algae from which you'll never extricate yourself.

79

'I didn't know Angelo had a strongbox,' she went on. 'He never mentioned it, and I never saw one in his apartment.'

Montalbano stared hard at the toe of his left shoe.

'Did you find it?' she continued.

'No. We found the keys but not the box. Doesn't that seem strange to you?'

'I suppose it does.'

'It's another thing that should have been in the apartment but wasn't.'

Michela gave a sign that she understood what Montalbano was getting at. She leaned her head back – she had a beautiful, Modiglianiesque neck – and looked at him through, fortunately, half-closed eyes. 'You're not thinking *I* took it?'

'Well, you see, I made a mistake.'

'What?'

'I left you alone at your brother's place that first night. I shouldn't have. You would have had all the time in the world to—'

'Take things away? Why would I do that?'

'Because you know a lot more about Angelo than we do.'

'Of course I do! We grew up together. We're brother and sister.'

'And therefore you're inclined to cover for him, even unconsciously. You told me that at one point your brother had decided to stop practising medicine. But that's not what happend. He was struck off.'

'Who told you that?'

'Elena Sclafani. I spoke to her this morning, before coming here.'

'Did she say why?'

'No. Because she didn't know. Angelo had only made vague mention of it to her, but since she wasn't interested, she didn't ask.'

'Ah, the poor little angel! She wasn't interested, but she was certainly in a rush to cast suspicion. She attacks, then looks the other way.'

She said this in a voice unfamiliar to the inspector, a voice that seemed produced not by vocal cords but by two sheets of sandpaper rubbed forcefully together.

'Well, why don't *you* tell me the reason?' he asked.

'Abortion.'

'Go on.'

'Angelo got an underage girl pregnant and, what was more, she was a patient of his. The girl, who was from a certain kind of family, didn't dare say anything at home and couldn't turn to any public institution. That left clandestine abortion the only option. Except that when the girl got home afterwards she suffered a violent haemorrhage. Her father accompanied her to the hospital and learned the whole story. Angelo assumed full responsibility.'

'What do you mean he "assumed full responsibility"? It seems clear to me that he *was* fully responsible!'

'No, he wasn't. He had asked a colleague of his, a friend from university days, to perform the abortion. The friend didn't want to, but Angelo managed to persuade him. When the story came out, my brother claimed he had done it, so he was reprimanded and struck off the medical register.'

'Tell me the girl's name and surname.'

'But, Inspector, it was more than ten years ago! She got married and no longer lives in Vigàta. Why do you want—'

'I'm not saying I want to interrogate her, but if it proves necessary, I'll do so with the utmost discretion, I promise.'

'Teresa Cacciatore. She married a contractor named Mario Sciacca. They live in Palermo and have a little boy.'

'Signora Sclafani told me she and your brother always met at his place.'

'That's right.'

'How is it you never crossed paths with her?'

'I didn't want to meet her. Not even by chance. I'd begged Angelo always to let me know when Elena was coming over.'

'Why didn't you want to meet her?'

'Antipathy. Aversion. Take your pick.'

'But you saw her only once!'

'Once was enough. Anyway, Angelo often talked about her.'

'What did he say?'

'That she had no equal in bed but was too money-hungry.'

'Did he pay her?'

'He used to buy her very expensive gifts.'

'Such as?'

'A ring. A necklace. A sports car.'

'Elena confided to me that she had made up her mind to leave him.'

'Don't believe it. She hadn't finished squeezing him. She was always making jealous scenes to keep him close.'

'Were you as hostile to Paola the Red?'

She leaped, literally, out of her armchair. 'Who — who told you about Paola?'

'Elena Sclafani.'

'The slut!' The sandpaper voice had returned.

'I'm sorry, but who are you referring to?' the inspector asked angelically. 'Paola or Elena?'

'Elena, for bringing her into this. Paola was ... is a sweet girl who fell sincerely in love with Angelo.'

'Why did your brother finish with her?'

'Their affair had gone on for too long ... He met Elena when he was tiring of her ... To Angelo Elena represented something new and intriguing that he couldn't resist, even though I ...'

'What's Paola's surname and her address?'

'Inspector! Do you expect me to give you personal information on all the women who had relationships with Angelo? On Maria Martino? Stella Lojacono?'

'Not all of them. Just those you mentioned.'

'Paola Torrisi-Blanco lives in Montelusa, Via Mille-fiori 26. She teaches Italian at the *liceo*.'

'Married?'

'No, but she would have been an ideal wife for my brother.'

'You knew her well?'

'Yes. We became friends. And we continued to see each other even after my brother broke up with her. I rang her this morning to tell her my brother had been murdered.'

'By the way, have any journalists contacted you?'

'No. Have they found out?'

'The story's starting to leak out. If they do, you should refuse to speak to them.'

'Of course.'

'Let me have the addresses, if you've got them, or the phone numbers of the other two women you remembered.'

'I don't have them to hand. I need to look in some old diaries. Is it all right if I give them to you tomorrow?'

'Perfectly.'

'Inspector, can I ask you something?'

'Go ahead.'

'Why are you centring your investigation on Angelo's women friends?'

Because you and Elena are doing nothing but serving me women's names on a platter — or, better, on a bed, he wanted to say, but didn't. 'You think it's a mistake?' he asked instead.

'I don't know whether or not it's a mistake. But there must be many other hypotheses one could make concerning the possible motive for my brother's murder.'

'Such as?'

'Oh ... something concerning his business — maybe an envious competitor ...'

At this point the inspector decided to lay a false card on the table. He put on an embarrassed air, as of someone who would like to say something but can't bring himself to do so.

'We favour the ... ahem ... the feminine trail because ...' He congratulated himself for coming up with the right words; even the British policeman's 'ahem' had emerged from his throat to perfection. He continued his masterly performance. '... a detail that perhaps I'd ... ahem ... better not ...'

'Tell me,' said Michela, assuming the air of someone expecting to hear the worst.

'Well, it's just that your brother, when he was killed, had just had ... er ... sex with a woman.'

It was a whopper: Pasquano had said something else. But he wanted to see if his words would have the same effect as they had the first time. They did.

The woman sprang to her feet. Her dressing-gown opened. She was naked underneath. No panties, no bra.

A splendid, lush, compact body. She arched her back. In the motion, her hair fell down on to her shoulders. She was clenching her fists, arms extended at her sides. Her eyes were popping out of her head. Fortunately they weren't looking at the inspector. Watching obliquely, as if through a window, Montalbano saw a raging sea in those eyes, with force-eight waves rising to peaks like mountains and crashing down in avalanches of foam, then re-forming and falling again. A memory from his school-days came back to him, of the terrible Erinyes. Then he thought the memory must be wrong: the Erinyes were old and ugly. Whatever, he clung to the arms of the chair in which he was seated. Michela was having trouble speaking. Her fury kept her teeth clenched.

'She did it!' The sheets of sandpaper had turned into grindstones. 'Elena killed him!'

Her chest had become a pair of bellows. Then, all at once, she fell backwards, hitting her head against the armchair and rebounding, then collapsing in a swoon.

Covered with sweat after the scene he'd just witnessed, Montalbano left the living room, saw a door ajar, realized it was the bathroom, went in, damped a towel, returned to the living room, knelt beside Michela and wiped her face. By now it had become a habit. Slowly she began to come round. When she opened her eyes, the first thing she did was cover herself with the dressing-gown.

'Feeling better?'

'Yes. Forgive me.'

She had amazing powers of recovery. She stood up. 'I'm going to get a drink of water.'

She returned and sat down, calm and cool, as though she hadn't just had an uncontrollable frightful bout of rage verging on an epileptic fit.

'Did you know that on Monday evening your brother and Elena were supposed to meet?'

'Yes. Angelo called to tell me.'

'Elena says that meeting never took place.'

'What was her story?'

'She said she went out, but after she got into the car she decided not to go to their rendezvous. She wanted to see if she could break off with your brother once and for all.'

'And you believe that?'

'She has an alibi, which I've checked.'

It was another whopping lie, but he wanted to avoid her flying into a rage if some journalist happened to mention Elena's name.

'Surely it's false.'

'You mentioned that Angelo used to buy Elena expensive gifts.'

'It's true! Do you think her husband, on *his* salary, can afford to buy her the kind of car she drives?'

'So, if that's the way it was, what motive would Elena have had for killing him?'

'Inspector, it was Angelo who wanted to end the relationship. He couldn't take it any longer. She tormented him with her jealousy. He told me she wrote to him once, threatening to kill him.'

'She sent him a letter?'

'Two or three.'

'Do you have them?'

'No.'

'We didn't find any letters from Elena in your brother's apartment.'

'He must have thrown them away.'

'I think I've kept you too long,' said Montalbano, standing up.

Michela also got to her feet. Suddenly she looked exhausted. She put a hand to her forehead and teetered.

'One last thing,' said the inspector. 'Did your brother like popular songs?'

'He listened to them now and then.'

'But there was no stereo or CD-player in his apartment.'

'He didn't listen to music at home.'

'Where did he, then?'

'In his car, during business trips. It kept him company. He had many cassettes.'

7

Michela had said her brother's garage was the first on the right. It had two locks, one on the left and one on the right-hand side of the rolling metal door. It didn't take the inspector long to find the key in the set he'd brought with him.

He opened the locks, then slipped a smaller key into another lock on the wall, turned it, and the door began to rise, too slowly for the inspector's curiosity. When it had opened all the way, Montalbano went in and immediately found the light switch. The fluorescent strip was bright, the garage spacious and in perfect order. At a glance, he ascertained that there was no strongbox in there and nowhere to hide one.

The car was a rather late-model Mercedes, one of those that are usually rented with a driver. In the compartment between the driver and passenger seats there were ten music cassettes. In the glovebox, he found the car's documents and a number of road maps. Just to be sure, he looked in the boot, which was sparkling clean, with a spare tyre, a jack and a red warning triangle.

A little disappointed, Montalbano repeated in reverse the complicated procedure he'd gone through to open the garage, then got back into his car and headed for Marinella.

It was nine fifteen in the evening and he wasn't hungry. He took off his clothes, slipped on a shirt and a pair of jeans and, barefoot, went out on to the veranda, then the beach.

The moonlight was so faint that the lights inside his house shone as brightly as if each room were illuminated not by lamps but by floodlights. Reaching the water's edge, he stood there for a few minutes, the sea splashing over his feet and the cool rising through his body to his head.

On the horizon he could see the glow of a few scattered night-fishing lamps. From far away, a plaintive female voice called twice: 'Stefanu! Stefanu!'

Lazily, a dog answered.

Motionless, Montalbano waited for the surf to enter his brain and wash it clean. At last the first light wave came like a caress, *swiiissh*, and carried away, *glugluglug*, Elena Sclafani and her beauty. Michela Pardo's tits, belly, arched body and eyes likewise disappeared. Once Montalbano the man was erased, all that should remain was the police inspector – a kind of abstract function, the individual who was supposed to solve the case and nothing more, no personal feelings involved. But as he was telling himself this, he knew perfectly well that he could never pull it off.

Back in the house, he opened the refrigerator. Adelina must have come down with an acute form of vegetarianism. *Caponata* and a sublime *pasticcio* of artichokes and spinach. He set the table on the veranda and wolfed the *caponata* as the *pasticcio* heated up. Then he revelled in the *pasticcio*. After clearing the table, he went to fetch Angelo's wallet from the plastic bag. He turned it upside-down, stuck his fingers into the different compartments and emptied it. Identity card. Driving licence. Tax code. Credit card from the Banca dell'Isola (*Can't you see you're losing it? Why didn't you look in the wallet straight away? You would have spared yourself the embarrassment with Michela.*) Two calling cards, one belonging to a Dr Benedetto Mammuccari, a surgeon from Palma; the other to one Valentina Bonito, a midwife from Fanara. Three postage stamps, two for the standard rate and one for priority mail. A photo of Elena in a topless swimsuit. Two hundred and fifty euros in fifties. The receipt from a full tank of petrol.

Enough. Stop.

All obvious, all normal. Too obvious, too normal for a man who was found shot in the face with his willy hanging out, whatever he'd used it for. OK, getting caught with your dick exposed no longer shocked anyone nowadays, and there had even been an honourable Member of Parliament, later to become a high charge of the state, who'd shown his to one and all in a photo printed in a number of glossy magazines. OK. But it was the two together – the whacking and the exposure – that made the case peculiar.

Or constituted the peculiarities of the case. Or, better yet, the whacking and the whack-off. Engrossed in these complex variations on the theme as he was putting everything back into the wallet, the inspector, when he got to the euros, suddenly stopped.

How much was in the account Michela had shown him? Roughly ninety thousand euros, of which fifty thousand were Michela's. Therefore Angelo had only forty thousand euros in the bank. Or scarcely eighty million lire, to use the old system. Something didn't add up. Angelo Pardo's earnings probably consisted of a percentage gained on the pharmaceutical products he placed. And Michela had suggested that her brother earned enough to live comfortably. OK, but was it enough to pay for the expensive presents that, according to Michela, he had given to Elena? Surely not. Today, going to market and buying food for a week, one spent as much as one used to do in a month. How did someone who didn't have a lot of money manage to buy jewellery and sports cars? Either Angelo was draining the bank account – which might explain Michela's resentment – or he had some other source of revenue, with a related bank account, of which there was no trace. And of which even Michela knew nothing. Or was she merely pretending to know nothing?

He went inside and turned on the television. Just in time for the late news on the Free Channel. His friend, the reporter Nicolò Zito, spoke first of an accident between a car and a truck that had killed four, then mentioned the murder of Angelo Pardo: the investigation had been assigned to the captain of the Montelusa Flying Squad. This explained why no journalists had come to harass Montalbano. It was clear poor Nicolò knew little or nothing about the case. He merely strung a couple of sentences together and moved on to another subject. So much the better.

Montalbano turned off the TV, phoned Livia for their customary evening greeting, which did not result in any squabbling this time – indeed, it was all kissy-kissy – and went to bed. No doubt thanks to the phone call, which had calmed him, he went straight to sleep, like a baby.

But the child woke up at two in the morning, and instead of starting to cry, like babies all over the world, he started to think.

His mind went back to his visit to the garage. He was convinced he'd neglected some detail. A detail that at the time had seemed unimportant but which he now felt was quite the reverse.

He reviewed, in his memory, everything he'd done from the moment he'd entered the garage to when he'd left. Nothing.

'I'll go back tomorrow,' he said to himself, and turned on to his side to go back to sleep.

Less than fifteen minutes later he was in his car, dressed higgledy-piggledy, and racing to Angelo Pardo's place, cursing like a maniac.

If the other tenants of that building seemed dead during the day, he could only imagine what they'd be like at three in the morning or thereabouts. Whatever, he took care to make as little noise as possible.

Having turned on the light in the garage, he began to study everything – empty jerry-cans, old engine-oil cans, pliers, monkey-wrenches – as though with a magnifying-glass. He found nothing worth considering. An empty jerry-can remained, desolately, a simple, empty jerry-can still stinking of petrol.

He moved on to the Mercedes. The road maps in the glove compartment didn't have any particular routes highlighted, and the car's documents were all in order. He lowered the sun visors, examined the cassettes one by one, stuck his hands into the side pockets, pulled out the ashtray, got out, opened the bonnet, saw only the engine beneath it. He went behind the car, opened the boot: spare tyre, jack, red triangle. He closed it.

He felt a kind of ever-so-light electric shock, and reopened the boot. Here was the detail he'd neglected.

A tiny paper triangle stuck out from under the rubber mat. He leaned forward: it was the corner of a linen-paper envelope. He slipped it out with two fingers. It was addressed to Signor Angelo Pardo, and Signor Angelo Pardo, after opening it, had put three letters, all addressed to him, inside it. Montalbano pulled out the first and looked at the signature. Elena. He put it back in the linen envelope, closed the car, turned off the garage lights, lowered the metal door and, the linen envelope in hand, headed back to his car, which he'd left a few yards from the garage.

'Stop! Thief!' yelled a voice that seemed to come from the heavens.

He stopped and looked up. On the top floor a window was open; against the light, the inspector recognized His Majesty Victor Emmanuel III, pointing a hunting rifle at him.

Was he going to start arguing with that raving lunatic at this hour of the night? When that guy got a bee in his bonnet, there was nothing to be done. Montalbano turned his back and walked away.

'Stop or I'll shoot!'

Montalbano kept walking, and His Majesty fired. Everyone knew, of course, that the last of the Savoys were notoriously trigger happy. Fortunately Victor Emmanuel was not a good shot. The inspector dived into his car, turned on the engine and drove off, screeching his tyres even worse than the cops in American movies, as a second shot ended up some thirty yards away.

As soon as he got home he started to read Elena's letters to Angelo. All three had the same two-part plot.

Part one consisted of a kind of passionate erotic delirium – clearly Elena had written the letters just after a particularly steamy encounter – where she remembered, with a wealth of detail, what they had done and how many orgasms she had had during Angelo's endless tric-troc.

Montalbano stopped, perplexed. Despite his personal experience and his readings of a variety of erotic classics, he didn't know what 'tric-troc' meant. Maybe it was a term from the sort of secret jargon that lovers always invent between themselves.

Part two, on the other hand, was in a completely different tone. Elena imagined that Angelo, when he went on his business trips to the different towns in the province, had girlfriends galore in each place, like those sailors who supposedly have a woman in every port. This drove her mad with jealousy. And she warned him: if she could ever prove that Angelo was cheating on her, she would kill him.

In the first letter, in fact, she claimed she had followed Angelo in her car all the way to Fanara, and she asked him a precise question: why had he stopped for an hour and a half at Via Libertà 82, seeing that there was neither a pharmacy nor a doctor's surgery at that address? Did another mistress of his live there? Whatever the case, Angelo would do well to remember that any betrayal meant sudden, violent death.

When he had finished reading the letters Montalbano wasn't entirely convinced. True, these letters proved Michela right, but they didn't correspond to the Elena he thought he'd met. It was as though they'd been written by a different person.

And, anyway, why would Angelo have kept them hidden in the boot of the Mercedes? Did he not want his sister to read them? Was he perhaps embarrassed by the first part of the letters, which told of his acrobatics between the sheets with Elena? That might explain it. But did it make sense that Elena, who was so attached to money, would murder the person who was giving her a great deal of it, if only in the form of presents?

Without realizing it, he grabbed the telephone. 'Hello, Livia? Salvo here. I want to ask you something. In your opinion, is it logical for a woman to kill a lover who lavishes her with expensive gifts just because she's jealous? What would you do?'

There was a long silence.

'Hello, Livia?'

'I don't know if I would kill a man out of jealousy, but if he woke me up at five o'clock in the morning, yes, I would,' said Livia.

And she hung up.

*

He got to work a bit late. He hadn't managed to fall asleep until around six, having tossed and turned with a

97

single thought lodged in his brain: namely, that according to the most elementary rules, he should have apprised Prosecutor Tommaseo of Elena Sclafani's situation. But he didn't want to. And the problem set his nerves on edge just enough to prevent him sleeping.

One look at his face was enough to tell the entire police station that this wasn't a good day.

In the cubby-hole somebody else was in Catarella's place: Minnitti, a Calabrese.

'Where's Catarella?'

'He stayed up all night working at the station, Chief, and this morning he collapsed.'

Maybe he'd taken Angelo Pardo's laptop home with him because there was no sign of it anywhere. The moment the inspector sat down at his desk, Fazio came in.

'Two things, Chief. The first is that Commendatore Ernesto Laudadio came here this morning.'

'And who is Commendatore Ernesto Laudadio?'

'You know him well, Chief. He's the man who called us when he got it into his head that you wanted to rape the murder victim's sister.'

So His Majesty Victor Emmanuel III went by the name of Ernesto Laudadio! And while he was earnestly lauding God, he was busting his fellow man's balls.

'What did he come for?'

'He wanted to report a crime committed by persons unknown. Apparently last night somebody tried to force open the victim's garage door, but the *commendatore* foiled the plot, firing two rifle shots at the unknown man and chasing him away.'

'Did he injure him?'

Fazio answered with another question. 'Are you injured, Chief?'

'No.'

'Then the *commendatore* didn't injure anyone, thank God. Would you please tell me what you were doing in that garage?'

'I'd gone earlier to look for the strongbox, since both you and I had forgotten to look there.'

'That's true. Did you find it?'

'No. I went back later because all at once a small detail came back to me.' He didn't tell him what this detail was, and Fazio didn't ask.

'And what was the second thing you wanted to tell me?'

'I got some information on Emilio Sclafani, the schoolmaster.'

'Oh, good, tell me.'

Fazio slipped a hand into his jacket pocket, and the inspector shot him a dirty look.

'If you pull out a piece of paper with the teacher's father's name, the teacher's grandfather's name, the teacher's father's grandfather's name, I'll—'

'Peace,' said Fazio, removing his hand from his pocket.

'Will you never rid yourself of this public records' vice?'

'Never, Chief. So, anyway, the schoolmaster is a repeat offender.'

'In what sense?'

'I'll explain. The man's been married twice. The first time, when he was thirty-nine and teaching at Comisini, to a nineteen-year-old girl, a former pupil of his from the *liceo*. Her name was Maria Coxa.'

'What kind of name is that?'

'Albanian. But her father was born in Italy. The marriage lasted exactly one year and three months.'

'What happened?'

'Nothing happened. At least, that's what people say. After being married a year, the bride realized it was mighty strange that every evening, when her husband lay down beside her, he would say, "Goodnight, my love", kiss her forehead, and go to sleep. Get my drift?'

'No.'

'Chief, our schoolmaster did not consummate.'

'Really?'

'So they say. And his very young wife, who needed to consummate—'

'Went consummating elsewhere.'

'Exactly, Chief. A colleague of her husband's, a gym teacher ... You get the idea. Apparently the husband found out, but didn't react. One day, however, he came home at an unexpected time of day and caught his wife trying out a particularly difficult exercise with his colleague. Things got nasty and reversed.'

'Reversed?'

'I mean our schoolmaster didn't touch his wife, but took it out on his colleague and beat him to a pulp. It's true the gym teacher was stronger and in better shape, but Emilio Sclafani put him in hospital. He went berserk. Something turned him from a patient cuckold into a wild beast.'

'What was the upshot?'

'The gym teacher decided not to press charges, Sclafani split up with his wife, had himself transferred to Montelusa and got a divorce. Now, in his second marriage, he finds himself in the same situation as he was in the first. That's why I called him a repeat offender.'

Mimì Augello walked in and Fazio walked out.

'What are you still doing here?' Mimì asked.

'Why? Where am I supposed to be?'

'Wherever you want, but not here. In fifteen minutes Liguori's going to be here.'

The idiot from Narcotics!

'I forgot! I'll just make a couple of phone calls and run.'

The first was to Elena Sclafani. 'Montalbano here. Good morning, Signora. I need to talk to you.'

'This morning?'

'Yes. Can I come round in half an hour?'

'I'm busy until one o'clock, Inspector. If you want, we can meet this afternoon.'

'I could make it this evening. But will your husband be there?'

'I've already told you that's not a problem. At any rate, he's coming back this evening. Oh, listen. I have an idea. Why don't you invite me out to lunch?'

They agreed on the time and place.

The second call was for Michela Pardo.

'I'm sorry, Inspector, I was just on my way out. I have to go to Montelusa to see Judge Tommaseo. Fortunately my aunt was able ... What is it?'

'Do you know Fanara?'

'The town? Yes.'

'Do you know who lives at Via Libertà 82?'

Silence, no answer.

'Hello, Michela?'

'Yes, I'm here. It's just that you took me by surprise ... Yes, I know who lives at Via Libertà 82.'

'Tell me.'

'My aunt Anna, my mother's other sister. She's para-lysed. Angelo is ... was very close to her. Whenever he went to Fanara he always dropped in to see her. But how did you know—'

'Routine investigation, I assure you. Naturally I have many other things to ask you.'

'You could come this afternoon.'

'I have a meeting with the commissioner. Tomorrow morning, if that's all right with you.'

He dashed out of the office, got into the car, and drove off. He decided he needed to have another look at Angelo's apartment. Why? Because. Instinct demanded it.

Inside the front door, he climbed the silent staircase of the dead house, and cautiously opened, without a sound, the door to Angelo's flat, terrified that His Majesty Victor Emmanuel III might burst out of his apartment with a dagger in his hand and stab him in the back. He headed to the study, sat down behind the desk and started to think.

As usual, he sensed that something didn't add up, but couldn't bring it into focus. So he got up and started walking round the flat, fussing about in each room. At one point he even opened the shutter to the balcony off the living room and went outside.

In the street in front of the building, a convertible had stopped, and two young people, a boy and a girl, were kissing. They had the radio — or whatever it was — at full volume.

Montalbano leaped backwards — not because he was scandalized by what he had seen but because he finally understood why he'd felt the need to return to the apartment.

He went back to the study, sat down, searched for the right key in Angelo's set, put it into the lock of the middle drawer, opened it, took out the little book entitled

The Most Beautiful Italian Songs of All Time, and started leafing through it.

'Pale little lady, sweet fifth-floor neighbour / from across the way . . .'

'Today the carriage may seem / a strange relic from the olden days . . . '

'Don't forget these words of mine / little girl, you don't know what love is . . . '

All the songs dated back to the nineteen forties and fifties. He, Montalbano, probably hadn't been born when people were singing them to themselves. And, more importantly – or so it seemed to him – they had nothing to do with the cassettes in the Mercedes, which were all rock music.

8

In the narrow white margin on each page of the booklet, numbers had been written. The first time he'd seen them, the inspector had thought they involved some sort of analysis of the metre. Now, however, he realized that the numbers referred only to the first two lines of each song. Next to the lines *Pale little lady, sweet fifth-floor neighbour / from across the way,* were the numbers 32 and 22 respectively; next to *Today the carriage may seem / a strange relic from the olden days,* 23 and 29; while *Don't forget these words of mine / little girl, you don't know what love is* had 26 and 31. And so on for all the other ninety-seven songs in the book. The answer came to him all too easily: those numbers corresponded to the total number of letters in the respective line of the song. A code, apparently. The hard thing was figuring out what it meant. He put the booklet into his pocket.

*

As he was about to enter the Trattoria da Enzo, Montalbano heard someone call him. He stopped and turned. Elena Sclafani was getting out of a sort of red missile, a convertible, which she had just parked. She was wearing a tracksuit and gym shoes, her long hair flowing on to her shoulders and held in place only by a light blue headband slightly above her forehead. Her blue eyes were smiling, and her red lips, which looked painted, were no longer pouting. 'I've never eaten here before. I've just come from the gym so I've got a hearty appetite.'

A wild animal, young and dangerous. Like all wild animals.

And, in the end, like all youth, the inspector thought, with a twinge of melancholy.

Enzo sat them at a table slightly apart from the others. But there weren't many people there, in any case. 'What would you like?' he asked.

'Is there no menu?' asked Elena.

'It's not the custom here,' said Enzo, looking at her disapprovingly.

'Would you like the seafood antipasto? It's excellent,' said Montalbano.

'I eat everything,' Elena declared.

The look Enzo gave her changed suddenly, turning not only benevolent but almost affectionate. 'Then leave it to me,' he said.

'There's a slight problem,' said Montalbano, who wanted to cover himself.

'What's that?'

'You suggested we go out to lunch together, and I was happy to accept. But...'

'Come on, out with it. Your wife—'

'I'm not married.'

'Something serious?'

'Yes.' Why was he answering her? 'The problem is that when I eat I prefer not to talk.'

She smiled. 'You're the one who's supposed to ask the questions. If you don't, then I don't have to answer. And, anyway, if you really must know, when I do something I like to do only that one thing.'

The upshot was that they gobbled up the antipasto, the spaghetti with clam sauce, and crispy fried mullet, all the while exchanging only inarticulate sounds along the lines of *ah*, *oh* and *um*, which varied only in intensity and colour. And a few times they said *oh oh* in unison, while looking at each other. When it was over, Elena stretched out her legs under the table, half closed her eyes and let out a deep sigh. Then, like a cat, she stuck out the tip of her tongue and licked her lips. She very nearly started purring.

The inspector had once read a short story by an Italian author that told of a country where making love in public was not considered scandalous but the most natural thing in the world, while eating in the presence of others was thought immoral because it was such an intimate thing. A question came into his head and almost made him laugh. Want to bet that before long, because of age, he would be content to take his pleasure from women merely by sitting at the same table and eating with them?

'So where do we go now to talk?' asked Montalbano.

'Have you things to do?'

'Not immediately.'

'I'll make another suggestion. Let's go to my place and I'll make you some coffee. Emilio's in Montelusa, as I think I've already told you. Did you bring your car?'

'Yes.'

'Then follow me so you can leave whenever you like.'

Keeping up with the missile was not easy. At a certain point Montalbano decided to forget it. He knew the way, after all. In fact, when he arrived, Elena was waiting for him at the front door, a gym bag hanging from her shoulder.

'That's a very nice car you've got,' said Montalbano, as they were going up in the lift.

'Angelo bought it for me,' the girl said, almost indifferently, as though she was talking about a packet of cigarettes or something of no importance.

She's trying to pull the rug out from under me, thought Montalbano, feeling angry either because he'd thought of a cliché or because the cliché corresponded exactly with the truth. 'It must have cost him a lot of money.'

'I think so. I need to sell it as soon as possible.'

She led him into the living room.

'Why?'

'Because it's too expensive for my budget. It consumes almost as much petrol as an aeroplane. You know, when Angelo gave it to me, I accepted it on one condition: that every month he would reimburse me for the cost of fuel and the garage. He'd already paid for the insurance.'

'And did he do as you asked?'

'Yes.'

'Tell me something, how did he reimburse you? By cheque?'

'No, cash.'

Damn. A lost opportunity to find out if Angelo had any other bank accounts.

'Listen, Inspector, I'm going to make coffee and get changed. In the meantime, if you want to freshen up...'

She led him to a small guest bathroom beside the dining room.

He took his time, shedding his jacket and shirt and sticking his head under the tap. When he returned to the living room she still wasn't back. She arrived five minutes later with the coffee. She'd had a quick shower and put on a big sort of housecoat that came half-way down her thighs. Nothing else. She was barefoot. Plunging out from under the red housecoat, her legs, which were naturally long, looked endless. They were sinewy, lively, like a dancer's or athlete's. And the best of it — as was immediately clear to Montalbano — was that there was no intent, no attempt to seduce him on Elena's part. She saw nothing improper in appearing like this in front of a man she barely knew. As though reading his mind, she said, 'I feel comfortable with you. At ease. Even though that shouldn't be the case.'

'Right,' said the inspector.

He felt comfortable himself. Too comfortable. Which wasn't good. Again it was Elena who came back to the matter at hand. 'So, about those questions . . .'

'Aside from the car, did Angelo give you any other presents?'

'Yes, and rather expensive ones, too. Jewellery. If you want, I can get it and show you.'

'There's no need, thanks. Did your husband know?'

'About the gifts? Yes. Anyway, something like a ring I could easily hide, but a car like that—'

'Why?'

She understood at once. She was dangerously intelligent. 'You've never given presents to a ladyfriend?'

Montalbano felt annoyed. Livia was never, not even by accident, supposed to enter the tawdry, sordid stories he investigated. 'You're leaving out one detail.'

'What?'

He wanted to be offensive. 'That those presents were a way of paying you for your services.'

He was prepared for every possible reaction on Elena's part, except for her to laugh.

'Maybe Angelo overestimated my "services", as you call them. I assure you I'm hardly in a class of my own.'

'Then let me ask you again: why?'

'Inspector, the explanation is very simple. Angelo gave me these presents over the last three months, starting with the car. I think I've already told you that he had lately been overcome by ... Well, in short, he'd fallen in love with me. He didn't want to lose me.'

'And what about you?'

'I think I've already told you this too. The more possessive he became, the more distant I grew. I can't stand being harnessed, among other things.'

Hadn't an ancient Greek poet written a love poem to a young Thracian filly who couldn't stand being harnessed? But this wasn't the time for poetry. Almost against his will, the inspector slipped a hand into his jacket pocket and extracted the three letters he'd brought with him. He put them on the table.

Elena looked at them, recognized them, and didn't seem the least bit troubled. She left them where they were. 'Did you find them in Angelo's apartment?'

'No.'

'Where, then?'

'Hidden in the boot of his Mercedes.'

Suddenly, three wrinkles: one on her forehead, two at the corners of her mouth. For the first time she seemed genuinely baffled. 'Why hidden?'

'Well, I wouldn't know. But I could venture a guess. Maybe Angelo didn't want his sister to read them. Certain details might have proved embarrassing to him, as you can imagine.'

'What are you saying, Inspector? There were no secrets between those two!'

'Listen, let's forget the whys and wherefores. I found these letters inside a linen envelope hidden under the mat in the boot. Those are the facts. But I have another question, and you know what it is.'

'Inspector, those letters were practically dictated to me.'

'By whom?'

'Angelo.'

What did this woman think? That she could make him swallow the first bullshit that came into her head? He stood up abruptly, enraged. 'I'll expect you at the station at nine o'clock tomorrow morning.'

Elena also stood up. She'd turned pale, her forehead shiny with sweat. Montalbano noticed she was trembling. 'No, please, not the police station.' She kept her head down, fists clenched, arms extended at her sides, a little girl grown up too fast, scared of being punished.

'We're not going to eat you at the station, you know.'

'No, no, please, I beg you.'

A thin little voice that had turned into little sobs. Would this girl ever stop astonishing him? What was so terrible about having to go to the station? As one does with small children, he put a hand under her chin and raised her head. Elena kept her eyes closed, but her face was bathed in tears.

'OK, no police station, but don't tell silly stories.'

He sat down again. She remained standing but drew closer to Montalbano until she was right in front of him, her legs touching his knees. What was she expecting? That he would ask her for something in exchange for not forcing her to go to the police station? Suddenly the smell of her skin reached his nostrils, leaving him a little dazed. He became afraid of himself.

'Go back to your chair,' he said sternly, feeling as if he'd suddenly turned into a school principal.

Elena obeyed. Now seated, she tugged at the housecoat with both hands in a vain attempt to cover her thighs a little. But as soon as she let go, it climbed back up, worse than before.

'So, what's this unbelievable story about Angelo dictating the letters to you?'

'I never followed him in my car. Among other things, when we started seeing each other it had been a year since I'd had one. I'd had a bad accident that left my car a wreck, totally unusable. And I didn't have enough money to buy another, not even an old one. The first of those three letters, the one where I say I followed him to Fanara, dates from four months ago — you can check the date — when Angelo hadn't yet given me the car. But just to make the story more believable, he told me to write that he'd gone to a certain house — I no longer remember the address — and that I'd become suspicious.'

'Did he tell you who lived there?'

'Yes, an aunt of his, his mother's sister, I think.'

She'd recovered her nerve, and was herself again. But why had the inspector's words so frightened her?

'Let's suppose for a minute that Angelo actually did get you to write those letters.'

'But it's true!'

'And for the moment I'll believe that. Apparently he asked you to write them so that someone else would read them. Who?'

'His sister Michela.'

'How can you be so sure?'

'Because he told me so. He would arrange for her to come across them as if by accident. That's why I was so surprised when you said he was keeping them hidden in the boot of the Mercedes. It's unlikely Michela would ever find them there.'

'What was Angelo trying to get out of her by having her read the letters? What, in the end, was the purpose? Did you ask him?'

'Of course.'

'And what was his explanation?'

'He gave me an extremely stupid one. He said they were supposed to prove to Michela that I was madly in love with him, as opposed to what she claimed. And I pretended to be satisfied with this, because deep down I didn't give a damn about the whole thing.'

'You think in fact there was a different reason?'

'Yes. To give him breathing space.'

'Can you explain?'

'I'll try. You see, Inspector, Michela and Angelo were very close to each other. From what I was able to find out, when their mother was well, Michela would often sleep at her brother's place. She'd go out with him, and knew at all times where he was. She controlled him. At some point Angelo must have got tired of this, or at least he needed more freedom of movement. So I, with my fake but overwhelming jealousy, became a good alibi, which allowed him to get around without always having his sister in tow. He got me to write the other two letters before he went away on a couple of trips, one to Holland, the other to Switzerland. They were probably pretexts to prevent his sister going with him.'

Did this explanation for writing the letters hold water? In its twisted, contorted way, like a mad alchemist's alembic, it did. Elena's conjecture as to the real purpose proved convincing.

'Let's set aside the letters for a moment. Since, in our investigation, we have to cast a wide net, we've—'

'May I?' she interrupted, gesturing towards the letters on the coffee-table.

'Of course.'

'Go on, I'm listening,' said Elena, taking a letter out of its envelope and beginning to read it.

'We've found out a few things about your husband.'

'You mean what happened during his first marriage?' she said, continuing to read.

Let alone the rug. This girl was pulling out the ground from under him.

Without warning she threw back her head and laughed.

'What do you find so amusing?'

'The tric-troc! What must you have thought?'

'I didn't think anything,' said Montalbano, blushing.

'It's just that I have a very sensitive belly-button and so . . .'

Montalbano turned fire-red. So she liked to have her belly-button kissed and tongued! Was she insane? Didn't she realize those letters could send her to jail for thirty years? Tric-troc indeed! 'To get back to your husband . . .'

'Emilio told me everything,' said Elena, setting down the letter. 'He lost his head over a former pupil of his, Maria Coxa, and married her, hoping for a miracle.'

'What sort of miracle, if I may ask?'

'Inspector, Emilio has always been impotent.'

The girl's frankness was as brutal to the inspector as a stone dropped from the sky straight on to his head. Montalbano opened and closed his mouth without managing to speak.

'Emilio hadn't told Maria anything. But after a while he couldn't find any more excuses to cover up his unfortunate condition. So they made an agreement.'

'Stop just for a minute, please. Couldn't the wife have asked for an annulment or a divorce? Everyone would have said she was right!'

'Inspector, Maria was extremely poor. Her family had gone hungry to put her through school. The agreement was better than a divorce.'

'What did it entail?'

'Emilio agreed to find her a man she could go to bed with. He introduced her to a colleague of his, the gym teacher, with whom he'd already spoken.'

Montalbano goggled. No matter how much he'd seen and heard in all his years with the police, these intricate matters of sex and infidelity never failed to astonish him. 'He offered him his *wife*?'

'Yes, but on one condition. That he be informed beforehand of the meetings between Maria and his colleague.'

'Good God! Why?'

'Because then it wouldn't seem to him like a betrayal.'

Of course. From a certain point of view, Emilio Sclafani's reasoning made perfect sense. After all, wasn't a guy named Luigi Pirandello from round there?

'How do you explain that the gym teacher very nearly lost his life?'

'Emilio was never told about that encounter. It was, well, secret. So he reacted like a husband catching his wife committing flagrant adultery.'

The rules of the game. Wasn't there a play of that title by the aforementioned Pirandello?

'May I ask you a personal question?'

'Of course. I'm not so prudish with you.'

'Did your husband tell you he was impotent before or after you married him?'

'Before. Me, he told before.'

'And you agreed anyway?'

'Yes. He said I could go with other men if I wanted to. Discreetly, of course, and provided I always informed him of everything.'

'And did you keep your promise?'

'Yes.'

Montalbano had the clear impression that this 'Yes' was a lie. But it didn't seem to be all that important whether Elena met someone secretly without telling her husband. It was her own business. 'Listen, Elena, I have to be more explicit.'

'Go ahead.'

'Why does a beautiful girl like you, who must have men constantly wooing and desiring her, marry a man who is not rich, much older than her and can't even—'

'Inspector, have you ever imagined yourself in a storm at sea, amid the waves, after your boat has sunk?'

'I don't have much imagination.'

'Try to make the effort. You've been swimming for a long time and you just can't go any further. You realize you're going to drown. Suddenly you find yourself beside an object that might keep you afloat. What do you do? You grab it. And it makes no difference to you whether it's a plank of wood or a liferaft with radar.'

9

'Was it really that bad?'

'Yes.'

Clearly she didn't want to discuss the subject. It was hard for her. But the inspector couldn't pretend it didn't matter. He couldn't let it slide. He needed to know everything past and present about the people associated with the murder victim. It was his job, even though it sometimes made him feel like an employee of the Inquisition. And he didn't like this one bit.

'How did you meet Emilio?'

'After the scandal in Comisini, Emilio went to live for a while in Fela. There, my father, who's his second cousin, talked to him about me and my situation, and the fact that he'd been forced to put me in a special children's home.'

'Drugs?'

'Yes.'

'How old were you?'

'Sixteen.'

'Why did you start?'

'You're asking me a specific question that has no specific answer. It's hard to explain why I started. Even to myself. There were probably many different things that contributed ... First of all, my mother's death, when I wasn't even ten. Then my father's utter inability to care about anyone, including my mother. And simple curiosity. The opportunity arises at a moment of weakness. Your boyfriend from school, whom you think you're in love with, pushes you to try ...'

'How long did you stay at the home?'

'A whole year, without interruption. Emilio came to see me three times. The first time with my father, so he could meet me. After that, he came alone.'

'And then?'

'I ran away. I got on a train and went to Milan. I met a lot of different men. I ended up with one who was forty. I got stopped twice by the police. The first time, they sent me home to my father, because I was a minor. But if living with him had been dramatic before, this time it became impossible. So I ran away again. I went back to Milan. When they stopped me the second time—'

She froze, turned pale, started trembling again and swallowed without speaking.

'That's enough,' said Montalbano.

'No. I want to explain why ... The second time, as the two policemen were taking me to the station in their car, I offered to make a deal with them. You can imagine what. At first they pretended not to be interested. 'You have to come down to the station,' they kept repeating. So I pleaded with them. And when I realized they were getting off on hearing me implore them, since they could do whatever they liked with me, I made a scene, started crying, got down on my knees, right there in the car. Finally they accepted and took me to a secluded place. It was ... terrible. They used me for hours, as never before. But the worst of it was their contempt, their sadistic desire to humiliate me ... In the end, one urinated in my face.'

'Please, that's enough,' Montalbano repeated softly.

He felt a profound sense of shame for being a man. He knew the girl was not making up her story. Unfortunately this sort of thing had happened before. But now he understood why, at the mere mention of 'police station', Elena had nearly fainted.

'Why did the police arrest you?'

'Prostitution.' She said it with perfect ease, without shame or embarrassment. It was one thing among so many others she had done.

'When we were desperate for money,' she went on, 'my boyfriend used to prostitute me. Discreetly, of course. Not on the streets. But there were raids, and I was caught twice.'

'How did you meet up with Emilio again?'

She gave a little smile that Montalbano didn't immediately understand.

'Inspector, at this point the story becomes like a comic strip, or a feel-good soap opera. Do you really want to hear it?'

'Yes.'

'I'd come back to Sicily about six months earlier. On my twentieth birthday I went into a supermarket with the intention of stealing something to celebrate. But the moment I looked round, my eyes met Emilio's. He hadn't seen me since my days at the children's home, but recognized me at once. And, strangely enough, I recognized him. What can I say? He's been with me ever since. He saw me through detox, had me taken care of. He's looked after me for five years with a devotion I can't put into words. Four years ago he asked me to marry him. And that's the story.'

Montalbano got up and put the letters back into his pocket. 'I have to go.'

'Can't you stay a little longer?'

'Unfortunately I have an appointment in Montelusa.'

Elena stood up, drew near to him, lowered her head slightly and, for a moment, rested her lips on his.

'Thanks,' she said.

＊

He'd scarcely entered the station when a sudden scream from Catarella paralysed him.

'Chief! I screeeewed 'em!'

'Who'd you screw, Cat?'

'The last word, Chief!'

Standing up in his little cubby-hole, Catarella looked like a dancing bear, hopping for joy on one foot, then the other.

'I got the last word! I writ it and it disappeared!'

'Come into my office.'

'Right, like straight away, Chief! But first I gotta print the files.'

Better get out of there. People walking in and out of the station were looking at them a bit aghast.

Before entering his office, he stuck his head into Augello's. And Mimì, oddly, was there. Apparently the kid was feeling OK. 'What did Liguori want this morning?'

'To sensitize us.'

'Which means?'

'We've got to aim higher.'

'Meaning?'

'We've got to go in deep.'

Montalbano suddenly lost patience. 'Mimì, if you don't start talking clearly, you know where I'm going to go in deep with you?'

'Salvo, apparently the upper spheres of Montelusa are not pleased with our contributions to the fight against drug-dealers.'

'What are they talking about? In the last month we've put six behind bars!'

'It's not enough, according to them. Liguori says what we do is just small potatoes.'

'So what's big potatoes?'

'Not limiting oneself to arresting a few dealers by chance but acting according to a precise plan, provided by him, of course, which will supposedly lead us to the suppliers.'

'But isn't that his responsibility? Isn't he head of Narcotics? Why's he coming here breaking our balls? Let him make his plan and, instead of giving it to us, his own men can carry it out.'

'Salvo, apparently, according to his investigations, one of the biggest suppliers is here in Vigàta. So he wants our help.'

Montalbano was staring at him, lost in thought. 'Mimì, this whole business stinks. We need to talk about it, but I don't have time just now. I have to take care of something with Catarella, then run off to Montelusa to see the commissioner.'

Catarella was waiting for him in the doorway to his office, still dancing like a bear. He came in behind him and put two printed pages on the desk. The inspector glanced at them and understood nothing. There was a string of six-figure numbers piled on top of each other, and each of these numbers corresponded to another number. For example:

$$213452 \quad 136000$$
$$431235 \quad 235000$$

and so on. He realized that to understand the matter he had to dispatch Catarella, whose little tribal dance was getting on his nerves. 'Well done! My compliments, Catarella!'

Now he changed from a bear into a peacock. But since he had no tail to spread, he raised and extended his arms, fanned his fingers and spun round.

'How did you find the password?'

'Ah, Chief, Chief! That dead man is so clever, he drove me crazy! The word was the name of the sister, the dead man's, who's called Michela, combined in combination wit' the day, month an' year of birth when she's born, his sister, I mean, the dead man's, but written wittout nummers, only litters.'

Since, in his delight at having found the solution, Catarella uttered the whole sentence in a single breath, the inspector had trouble understanding, but grasped as much as he needed to.

'I think I remember you saying you needed three passwords.'

'Yessir, Chief, I do. Iss ongoing work.'

'Good, then go on working. And thanks again.'

Catarella staggered visibly.

'You dizzy?'

'A little, Chief.'

'You feel all right?'

'Yessir.'

'So why are you dizzy?'

''Cause you jes' gave me tanks, Chief.'

He walked out of the room as if he were drunk.

Montalbano cast another glance at the two sheets of paper. But since it was already time to go to Montelusa, he slipped them into the pocket that held the little songbook. Which he could have sworn contained the code for making some sense of all those numbers.

✻

'My dear Inspector! How goes it? Everyone doing well at home?'

'Fine, fine, Dr Lattes.'

'Make yourself comfortable.'

'Thank you, Doctor.'

He sat down. Lattes looked at him and he looked at Lattes. Lattes smiled and so did he.

'To what do we owe the pleasure of your visit?'

Montalbano's jaw dropped. 'Actually, I ... The commissioner told me ...'

'You're here for the meeting?' Lattes asked, in wonderment.

'Well, yes.'

'What? You mean the receptionist there, Cavarella –'

'Catarella.'

' – didn't tell you? I called late this morning to inform you that the commissioner had to leave for Palermo and that he'll expect to see you here tomorrow at this same hour.'

'Nobody told me anything.'

'But that's very serious! You must take measures!'

'I will, Doctor, don't you worry about that.'

What fucking measures could one possibly take against Catarella? It would be like trying to teach a crab to walk straight.

Since he was already in Montelusa, he decided to drop in on his friend Nicolò Zito, the reporter. He pulled up in front of the Free Channel studios, and the moment he walked in, the secretary told him Zito had fifteen free minutes before he went on the air.

'I haven't heard from you for a while,' Nicolò reproached him.

'Sorry, I've been busy.'

'Is there anything I can do for you?'

'No, Nicolò. I just wanted to see you.'

'Listen, are you giving Giacovazzo a hand in the investigation into Angelo Pardo's murder?'

It was nice of the Flying Squad captain not to have denied that the investigation had been turned over to him. This spared Montalbano from being besieged by journalists. But it was still hard for him to lie to his friend.

'No, no hand at all. You know what Giacovazzo's like. Why do you ask?'

'Because nobody can drag a single word out of him.'

Naturally. The captain of the Flying Squad wasn't talking to journalists because he had nothing to say.

'And yet,' Zito went on, 'I think that, considering what's happening now, he must have some idea.'

'Why? What's happening now?'

'Don't you read the papers?'

'Not always.'

'A nationwide investigation has led to the arraignment of more than four thousand doctors and pharmacists.'

'OK, but what's that got to do with it?'

'Salvo, use your brain! What did former doctor Angelo Pardo do for a living?'

'He was a representative for pharmaceutical concerns.'

'Exactly. And the charges being levelled at these doctors and pharmacists are collusion and kickbacks.'

'Meaning?'

'Meaning the doctors and pharmacists let themselves be corrupted by some pharmaceutical informers. In exchange for money or other gifts, those doctors and pharmacists would choose and prescribe medications indicated by the informers. And when they did this, they were handsomely rewarded. You see how it works now?'

'Yes. The informers didn't limit themselves to informing.'

'Exactly. Of course, not all doctors are corrupt, and not all informers are corrupters, but the phenomenon has proved very widespread. And, naturally, some very powerful pharmaceutical firms are implicated.'

'And you think that may be why Pardo was murdered?'

'Salvo, do you realize what kind of interests are

behind a set-up like this? But I don't think anything. All I'm saying is it's a lead that might be worth pursuing.'

✤

All things considered – the inspector reflected, as he drove back to Vigàta at five miles per hour – the visit to Montelusa had not been in vain. Nicolò's suggestion was one path that hadn't remotely occurred to him, but which had to be taken into consideration. But how to proceed? Open up Angelo Pardo's big diary – the one with the names, addresses and telephone numbers of doctors and pharmacists – pick up the receiver, and ask: 'Excuse me, but did you by any chance let yourself be corrupted by the pharmaceutical representative Angelo Pardo?'

That approach surely would not get any results. Maybe he needed to ask for a helping hand from the people who knew about this sort of investigation.

Back in his office, he called the headquarters of the Finance Police of Montelusa. 'Inspector Montalbano here. I'd like to speak with Captain Aliotta.'

'I'll put the major on straight away.'

Apparently he'd been promoted.

'My dear Montalbano!'

'Congratulations. I didn't know you'd been promoted.'

'Thanks. It was a year ago.'

An implicit reproach. Translation: *Cornuto, it's been a year since I last heard from you.*

'I wanted to know if Marshal Laganà is still on the job.'

'For a little while yet.'

'Since he once helped me considerably, I wanted to ask him if he could again, with your permission, of course . . .'

'Absolutely. I'll put him on. He'll be delighted.'

'Laganà? How's it going? Listen, could I have half an hour of your time? Yes? You don't know how grateful I am. No, no, I'll come to you in Montelusa. Is tomorrow evening around six thirty all right?'

The moment he hung up, Mimì Augello walked in with a gloomy face.

'What's wrong?'

'Beba called and said Salvuccio seems a bit agitated.'

'You know something, Mimì? It's you and Beba who are agitated, and if you keep getting agitated like this, you're going to drive the kid insane. For his first birthday I'm going to buy him a tiny little made-to-measure strait-jacket, so he can get used to it from an early age.'

Mimì didn't appreciate the remark. His face went from gloomy to downright black. 'Let's talk about some-thing else, all right? What did the commissioner want?'

'We didn't meet. He had to go to Palermo.'

'Explain to me why this business of Liguori coming here smells fishy to you.'

'Explaining a sensation is not easy.'

'Try.'

'Mimì, Liguori descends on us after Senator Nicotra dies in Vigàta – from drugs, though we're not supposed to say so. You yourself thought the same thing, if I remember correctly. Two others died before Nicotra, but they race over here only after the senator snuffs it. My question is: for what purpose?'

'I don't understand,' said Augello, confused.

'I'll be clearer. These guys want to find out who it was that sold the – let's say – "tainted" stuff to the senator, to prevent other people, bigwigs like the senator, coming to the same end. They've obviously been put under pressure.'

'And don't you think they're right to do what they're doing?'

'Absolutely right. It's just that there's a problem.'

'What?'

'Officially, Nicotra died of natural causes. Therefore whoever sold him the stuff is not responsible for his death. If we arrest him, it will come out that the guy sold his drugs not only to the senator but to a whole slew of the senator's playmates – politicos, businessmen and other high rollers. A scandal. A big mess.'

'So?'

'So when we arrest him and all hell breaks loose, we'll get swept up in it too. We who arrested him, not Liguori and company. People will come and tell us we should have proceeded more cautiously. Others will accuse us of acting like the judges in Milan, all Communists seeking to destroy the system ... In short, the commissioner and Liguori will have covered their arses but ours will look like the Mont Blanc tunnel.'

'So what should we do?'

'We? Mimì, Liguori spoke to *you*, who are the commissioner's rising star. I've nothing to do with it.'

'OK. What should I do?'

'Stick to the finest tradition.'

'Which is?'

'Armed conflict. You were getting ready to arrest the guy when he opened fire. You reacted and were forced to kill him.'

'Get out of here!'

'Why?'

'First of all, because that kind of reaction is not my style, and second, because nobody's ever heard of a drug-dealer, even a big fish, trying to avoid arrest by shooting his way out.'

'You're right. So, still in keeping with tradition, you arrest him but don't immediately turn him over to the judge. You let everyone know discreetly that you're keeping him here for two days. On the morning of the third day, you have him transferred to prison. Meanwhile the others will have had all the time in the world to get organized, and all you'll have to do is sit and wait.'

'For what?'

'For the dealer to get served coffee in prison. Good coffee. Like the coffee they gave Pisciotta and Sindona.

That way, the accused will clearly no longer be able to supply a list of his clients. And they all lived happily ever after. And that's the end of my story.'

Mimì, who until that moment had been standing, suddenly sat down. 'Let's think rationally about this.'

'Not now. Think about it tonight. In any case, Salvuccio will be keeping you awake. We'll talk about it again tomorrow morning with fresh minds. It's better this way. Now buzz off, 'cause I've got a phone call to make.'

Augello left, doubtful and dazed.

'Michela? Montalbano here. Would you mind if I dropped in on you for five minutes? No, no news. Just for ... All right, I'll be there in fifteen minutes.'

10

He buzzed the intercom, went in and climbed the stairs. Michela was waiting for him in the doorway. She was dressed as she had been on the first day Montalbano had met her.

'Good evening, Inspector. Didn't you say you couldn't come today?'

'I did, but my meeting with the commissioner was cancelled so . . .'

Why didn't she invite him in?

'How's your mother?'

'Better, given the circumstances. Enough that she let my aunt persuade her to go and stay with her.'

She couldn't bring herself to invite him in.

'I wanted to tell you that a friend of mine came to see me, knowing I was here alone. She's inside. I could send her away, if you want, but since I have nothing to hide, you can pretend she isn't there.'

'Are you saying I can speak openly in front of her?'

'Exactly.'

'Well, for me it's not a problem.'

Only then did Michela stand aside to let him in. The first thing the inspector saw as he entered the living room was a mass of red hair.

Paola the Red! he said to himself. Angelo's girlfriend before Elena.

On close examination, Paola Torrisi-Blanco was forty-ish, but at first glance she could easily have passed for ten years younger. A good-looking woman, no doubt about that. Which proved that Angelo liked them prime quality.

'If I'm in the way...' said Paola, standing up and extending her hand to the inspector.

'Not at all!' Montalbano said ceremoniously. 'Among other things, it saves me a trip to Montelusa.'

'Oh, really? Why?'

'I was planning to have a little chat with you.'

They all sat down and exchanged silent, polite smiles. A grand old get-together among friends. After an appropriate pause, the inspector turned to Michela. 'How did it go with Judge Tommaseo?'

'Don't remind me! That man is a ... He's got only one thing on his mind ... Some of the questions he asks ... It's so embarrassing.'

'What did he ask you?' Paola asked mischievously.

'I'll tell you later,' said Michela.

Montalbano imagined the scene: Tommaseo lost in

Michela's ocean eyes, red-faced, short of breath, trying to picture the shape of her tits under her penitent's frock and asking her, 'Do you have any idea why your brother's organ was completely exposed while he was being murdered?'

'Did Tommaseo say when you can hold the funeral?'

'Not for another three days. Is there any news?'

'On the investigation? For the moment it's at a stand-still. I came to see you to try to get it going again.'

'I'm at your disposal.'

'Michela, if you remember, when I asked you how much your brother earned, you said he brought home enough to maintain three people and two apartments fairly well. Is that right?'

'Yes.'

'Could you be more precise?'

'It's not easy, Inspector. He didn't have a fixed income or monthly salary. His earnings varied. There was a guaranteed minimum, as well as the reimbursement of expenses and a percentage on the products he managed to sell. Naturally, what really affected things, and in a positive way, was the commission. Now and then there were also productivity bonuses. But I wouldn't know how to translate all that into actual figures.'

'I have to ask you a delicate question. You told me Angelo used to give Elena very expensive gifts. This was confirmed to me by—'

'The whore?' Michela finished his sentence.

'Now, now!' said Paola, laughing.

'Why shouldn't I call her that?'

'It doesn't seem to be the case.'

'But for a while she actually was one! Inspector, when Elena was still a child, she ran away to Milan—'

'I know the whole story,' the inspector cut her short.

Though Elena might have confided in Angelo about the errors of her youth, it was unlikely he had communicated them to his sister. Apparently Michela was not above hiring some agency to dig up information on her brother's lover.

'In any case, he never gave *me* any gifts,' Paola said, at this point. 'Actually, no. Once he bought me a pair of earrings at a pavement booth in Fela. Three thousand lire, I remember. We didn't have the euro then.'

'Let's get back to the subject I'm interested in,' said Montalbano. 'To buy those gifts for Elena, did Angelo take money from your joint account?'

'No,' Michela said firmly.

'So where did he get it?'

'Whenever he got cheques for incentives or bonuses, he would cash them and keep the money at home. Once he had a certain amount, he would buy a present for that—'

'So you rule out the possibility that he could have had a personal account in some bank without your knowledge?'

'Absolutely.'

Prompt, firm, decisive. Maybe too prompt, too firm, too decisive.

How was it she never had the slightest doubt? Or maybe she had, and it wasn't so slight, but since it might cast some suspicion, some shadow, on her brother, she had decided it was better to deny it.

Montalbano tried to outflank her defences. He turned to Paola. 'You just said Angelo once bought you a pair of earrings in Fela. Why in Fela? Had you accompanied him there?'

Paola gave a little smile. 'Unlike Elena, I used to go with him on his rounds in the province.'

'He didn't take *her* because she was already following him!' Michela let fly.

'When I was free of commitments at school, of course,' Paola continued.

'Did you ever see him go into a bank?'

'Not that I can remember.'

'Was he very friendly with any of the doctors or pharmacists he used to visit?'

'I don't understand the question.'

'Were there any of his ... let's call them clients, with whom he was a little friendlier than with others?'

'Inspector, I didn't know them all. He used to introduce me as his girlfriend. And in a way it was true. But it seemed to me that he treated them all the same.'

'When he took you with him, were you present at all his meetings?'

'No, sometimes he would tell me to wait in the car or go for a walk.'

'Did he ever give a reason?'

'Well, he used to joke about it. He'd say he had to see a handsome young doctor and he was afraid that ... or he would explain that the doctor was a very devout, narrow-minded Catholic who might not approve of my presence...'

'Inspector,' Michela cut in, 'my brother clearly distinguished his friends from the people he did business with. I don't know if you noticed, but in his desk he kept two diaries, one with the addresses of friends and family, the other with—'

'Yes, I noticed,' said Montalbano. Then, still speaking to Paola: 'You, apparently, teach at the *liceo* of Montelusa?'

'Yes. Italian.' She gave another little smile. 'I see what you're getting at. Emilio Sclafani is not just my colleague. In a way we're friends. One evening I invited Emilio and his young wife to dinner. Angelo was there too, and that's when it began between them.'

'Listen, Elena told me her husband knew about her affair with Angelo. Can you by any chance confirm that?'

'It's true. In fact, the strangest thing happened.'

'Namely?'

'It was Emilio himself who told me that Angelo and his wife had become lovers. She'd told him just a few hours before. I didn't want to believe it. I thought Emilio was pulling my leg. The next day Angelo phoned me to say that he wouldn't be able to see me for a while. So I blew up and told him what Emilio had told me. He stammered a bit, then owned up to it. But he pleaded with me to be patient, said it was just a little fling ... But I was adamant, and our relationship ended there.'

'You never saw each other again?'

'No. We never spoke again, either.'

'And did you maintain friendly relations with Mr Sclafani?'

'Yes. But I never invited him to dinner again.'

'Have you seen him since Angelo died?'

'Yes. Even this morning.'

'How did he seem?'

'Upset.'

Montalbano hadn't expected such a prompt reply. 'In what way?'

'Don't get the wrong idea, Inspector. Emilio's upset because his wife lost her lover, that's all. Elena probably confessed to him how attached she was to him, how jealous—'

'Who told you she was jealous? Emilio?'

'Emilio has never said anything to me about Elena's feelings towards Angelo.'

'It was me,' Michela cut in.

'She also gave me a sort of summary of Elena's letters.'

'Speaking of which, have you found them?' asked Michela.

'No,' said Montalbano, lying.

On this matter, he sensed intuitively, in his gut, that the more he muddied the waters the better.

'She obviously got rid of them,' Michela said, convinced.

'What for?' the inspector asked.

'What do you mean, what for?' Michela reacted. 'Those letters could be used as evidence against her!'

'But, you know,' Montalbano said, with an innocent, angelic look on his face, 'Elena has already admitted writing them. Jealousy and death threats included. If she admits this, what reason would she have to get rid of them?'

'Well, then, what are you waiting for?' said Michela, summoning her special sandpaper voice.

'To do what?'

'Arrest her!'

'There's a problem. Elena says those letters were practically dictated to her.'

'By whom?'

'Angelo.'

The two women reacted entirely differently.

'Slut! Bitch! Liar!' Michela screamed, springing to her feet.

Paola sank further into her armchair. 'What could have possessed Angelo to make her write him jealous letters?' she asked, more curious than confused.

'Even Elena couldn't tell me,' said Montalbano, lying again.

'She couldn't tell you because it's totally untrue!' Michela said, practically screaming.

Her voice was turning dangerously from sandpaper into the two grindstones. Having no desire whatsoever to witness another scene from a Greek tragedy, Montalbano thought he could be satisfied with the evening's proceedings. 'Did you write down those addresses for me?' he asked Michela.

The woman looked at him in confusion.

'Remember? The two women, one of whom, I think, was named Stella . . .'

'Oh, right. Just a minute.' She left the room.

Then Paola, leaning slightly forward, said to him softly, 'I need to talk to you. Could you call me tomorrow morning? There's no school. I'm in the phone book.'

Michela returned with a sheet of paper, which she handed to the inspector. 'The list of Angelo's past loves.'

'Is there anyone I don't know about?' asked Paola.

'I don't think Angelo hid any of his amorous history from you.'

Montalbano stood up, and it was time for fond good-byes.

*

It had become so humid that there was no point in staying out on the veranda, even though it was covered.

The inspector went inside and sat at the table. His brain, after all, functioned in the same way inside or outside. For the past half-hour, in fact, a lively debate had been raging inside him.

The theme was: during an investigation, does a real policeman take notes or not?

He, for example, had never done so. Not only that, it irritated him when others did, even if they were better policemen than he.

But that was in the past. Because for a while now he'd been feeling the need to do so. And why did he feel the need to do so? Elementary, my dear Watson. Because he realized he was starting to forget some very important things. Alas, old friend, good Inspector, it's now *los cinco de la tarde*, and we've touched the sore spot of the whole matter. One starts to forget things when the weight of years begins to make itself felt. What was it, more or less, a poet once said?

> How the snow weighs down the branches
> and the years stoop the shoulders so dear;
> the years of youth are faraway years.

Perhaps it was better to change the title of the debate: during an investigation, does an *old* policeman take notes or not?

By adding age to the equation, taking notes seemed less unbecoming to Montalbano. But this implied unconditional surrender to the advancing years. He had to find a compromise. Then a brilliant idea came to him. He picked up paper and pen and wrote himself a letter.

Dear Inspector Montalbano,

I realize that at this moment your cojones are in a dizzying spin for entirely personal reasons concerning the idea of old age stubbornly knocking on your door, but I am pleased to remind you, with the present letter, of your duties, and would like to present you with a few observations on the ongoing investigation into the murder of Angelo Pardo.

First. Who was Angelo Pardo?
    A former doctor struck off the Medical Association register owing to an abortion involving a girl made pregnant by him (absolutely must talk to Teresa Cacciatore who lives in Palermo).
    He begins working as a medical/pharmaceutical 'informer', earning much more than he tells his sister. In fact, he lavishes extremely expensive gifts on his last mistress, Elena Sclafani.
    He very likely has a bank account somewhere, which we have not yet managed to locate.
    He most certainly owned a strongbox that has never been found.
    He was murdered by a gunshot to the face (is this significant?).
    At the moment of death, moreover, his cock was hanging out

(this certainly is significant, but exactly what does it signify?).

Possible motives for the murder:

a) *female troubles;*

b) *shady influence-peddling and kickbacks, a lead suggested by Nicolò and possibly worth pursuing* (check with Marshal Laganà).

He uses a secret code (for what?).

He has three computer files protected by passwords. The first of these, which Catarella succeeded in opening, is entirely in code.

Which means that Angelo Pardo definitely had something he wanted to keep carefully hidden.

One last note: why were the three letters from Elena hidden under the mat in the boot of the Mercedes? (I have a feeling this point is of some importance, but I can't say why.)

Please forgive me, dear Inspector, if this first section, devoted to the murder victim, is a bit disorganized, but I wrote these things down as they came into my head, not according to any logical sequence.

Second, Elena Sclafani.

You're wondering, naturally, why I wrote Elena Sclafani's name second. I realize, my friend, that you've taken quite a shine to the girl. She's pretty (OK, gorgeous — I don't mind you correcting me), and of course you would do everything in your power to keep her off the top of the list of suspects. You like the sincere way she talks about herself, but has it never occurred to you that sincerity can sometimes be a deliberate strategy for

*leading one away from the truth, just like the apparently opposite
strategy, that is, lying? You think I'm talking philosophy?*

OK, then, I'll brutally play the cop.

*There is no question that there are letters from Elena in
which, out of jealousy, she makes death threats to her lover.*

*Elena admits to having written these letters, but claims they
were dictated to her by Angelo. There is no proof of this, however;
it is only an assertion with no possibility of verification. And the
explanations she gives for why Angelo made her write them are,
you must admit, dear Inspector, rather fuzzy.*

For the night of the murder, Elena has no alibi. (Careful:
you were under the impression she was hiding
something, don't forget!) *She says she went out driving
in her car, with no precise destination, for the sole purpose
of proving to herself that she could do without Angelo. Does
her lack of an alibi for that evening seem like nothing to
you?*

*As for Elena's blind jealousy, there are not only the letters
to attest to this, but also Michela's testimony. Debatable
testimony, true, but it will carry weight in the eyes of the public
prosecutor.*

*Would you like me to describe a scenario, dear Inspector,
that you will surely find unpleasant? Just for a moment, pretend
that I am Prosecutor Tommaseo.*

*Wild with jealousy and now certain that Angelo is being
unfaithful to her, Elena, that evening, arms herself — where and
how she obtained the weapon we'll find out later — and goes and
waits outside Angelo's building. But first she calls her lover to*

tell him she can't come to his place. Angelo swallows the bait, brings the other woman home and, to be on the safe side, takes her up to the room on the terrace. For reasons we may or may not discover, the two do not make love. But Elena doesn't know this. And in any case this detail is, in a way, of no consequence. When the woman leaves, Elena enters the building, goes up to the terrace, quarrels or does not quarrel with Angelo, and shoots him. And, as a final outrage, she zips open his jeans and exposes the bone, as it were, of contention.

This reconstruction, I realize, is full of holes. But do you somehow expect Tommaseo not to revel in it? Why, the man will dive into it head first.

I'm afraid your Elena's in quite a pickle, old boy.

And you, if I may say so, are not doing your duty, which would be to tell the public prosecutor how things stand. And the worst of it — given the unfortunate circumstance that I know you very well — is that you have no intention of doing it. Your duty, that is.

All I can do, therefore, is take note of your deplorable, and partisan, course of action.

The only path left is to find out, as quickly as possible, the meaning of the code contained in the little songbook — what it refers to, and what the hell the first file opened by Catarella means.

Third. Michela Pardo.

Despite the woman's manifest inclination towards Greek tragedy, you do not consider her, as things now stand, capable of *fratricide. It is beyond all doubt, however, that Michela is ready to do anything to keep her brother's name from being sullied. And she certainly knows more about Angelo's dealings than she lets on. Among other things, you, distinguished friend, suspect that Michela, taking advantage of your foolishness, may have removed something crucial to the case from Angelo's apartment.*

But I'll stop here.
With best wishes for success, I remain,
Yours sincerely,

Salvo Montalbano

11

The following morning the alarm clock rang and Montalbano woke up, but instead of racing out of bed to avoid unpleasant thoughts of old age, decrepitude, Alzheimer's and death, he just lay there.

He was thinking of the distinguished schoolmaster Emilio Sclafani, whom he'd not yet had the pleasure of meeting personally in person, but who nevertheless deserved to be taken into consideration. Yes, the good professor was definitely worthy of a little attention.

First, because he was an impotent man with a penchant for marrying young girls – whether in first or second blush, it didn't matter – who could have been, in both cases, his daughters. The two wives had one thing in common, which was that meeting the schoolmaster had helped them to pull themselves out of difficult situations, to say the least. The first wife was from a family of ragamuffins, while the second was losing her way down a black hole of prostitution and drugs. By marrying them, the schoolmaster was, first and foremost, securing their gratitude. We want to call a spade a spade, don't we? The professor was subjecting them to a sort of indirect blackmail: he would rescue them from their poverty or confusion on the condition that they remained with him, even while knowing his shortcomings. Such kindness and understanding, as Elena said! Anything but.

Second, the fact that he himself had chosen the man with whom his first wife might satisfy her natural, young-womanly needs was in no way a sign of generosity. It was, in fact, a refined way to keep her even more tightly on a leash. And it was, among other things, a way to fulfil, as they say, his conjugal duty through a third party appointed by him for such a purpose. The wife, more-over, was supposed to inform him every time she met the lover and even describe the encounter to him in detail afterwards. Indeed, when the schoolmaster surprised them during an encounter about which he had not been informed, things had turned nasty.

After his experience with his first wife, the school-master allowed the second wife freedom of masculine choice, without prejudice to the obligation of prior notification of the day and time of mounting (could you really put it any other way?).

But why, knowing his natural deficiency, did the dis-tinguished professor want to get married twice?

Perhaps the first time he'd hoped that a miracle, to use Elena's word, would occur, so we'll leave it at that.

But the second time? How is it he hadn't become more savvy? Why didn't he marry, for example, a widow of a certain age whose sensual needs had already been abundantly mollified? Did he need to smell the fragrance of young flesh beside him in bed? Who did he think he was? Mao Tse-tung?

Anyway, his talk the night before with Paola the Red (speaking of whom, he mustn't forget she wanted him to call her) had brought out a contradiction that might or might not prove important. Namely, Elena maintained she had never wanted to go out to dinner or to the movies with Angelo, to prevent people laughing at her husband behind his back, While Paola said that she'd learned of the relationship between Elena and Angelo from the schoolmaster himself. Thus: while the wife was doing everything she could to keep her hanky-panky from becoming the talk of the town, her husband didn't hesitate to state flat out that she was engaging in hanky-panky.

The schoolmaster, moreover, had, according to Paola, seemed upset about the violent death of his wife's lover. Does that seem right?

He got up, drank his coffee, had a shower and shaved, but as he was about to leave, a wave of lethargy swept over him. All of a sudden he no longer felt like going to the office, seeing people, talking.

He went out on to the veranda. The day looked as if it was made of porcelain. He decided to do what his body was telling him to do. 'Catarella? Montalbano here. I'll be coming in late today.'

'Aah, Chief, Chief, I wannet a say—'

He hung up, grabbed the two sheets of paper Catarella had printed out and the little songbook, then laid them on the table on the veranda.

He went back inside, looked in the phone book, found the number he wanted and dialled it. As it rang, he checked his watch: nine o'clock, just the right time to call a schoolteacher on a weekend.

Montalbano let the phone ring for a long time and was about to lose patience when he heard someone pick up at the other end.

'Hello?' said a male voice, sounding slightly groggy.

The inspector hadn't expected this and felt a little bewildered.

'Hello?' the male voice repeated, now not only slightly groggy but also slightly irritated.

'Inspector Montalbano here. I would like—'

'You want Paola?'

'Yes, if it's not—'

'I'll get her.'

Three minutes of silence passed.

'Hello?' said a female voice the inspector didn't recognize.

'Am I speaking with Paola Torrisi?' he asked, doubtful.

'Yes, Inspector, it's me. Thanks for calling.'

But it wasn't the same voice as the previous evening. This one was a bit husky, deep and sensual, like that of someone who ... Suddenly he realized that maybe nine o'clock in the morning wasn't the right time of day to call a schoolteacher who, not at work, was busy with other things. 'I'm sorry if I've inconvenienced you ...'

She giggled. 'It's no big deal. I want to tell you something, but not over the phone. Could we meet somewhere? I could drop in at the station.'

'I won't be in my office this morning. We could meet later, in Montelusa. You tell me where.'

They decided on a café on the Promenade. At noon. That way Paola could finish at her own pace what she had started before she was interrupted by his phone call. And maybe even allow herself an encore.

While he was at it, he decided to confront Dr Pasquano. Better over the phone than in person.

'What's the story, Doctor?'

'Take your pick. *Little Red Riding Hood* or *Snow White and the Seven Dwarfs.*'

'No, Doctor, I meant—'

'I know what you meant. I've already let Tommaseo know that I've done what I was supposed to do and that he'll have the report by tomorrow.'

'What about me?'

'Ask Tommaseo to give you a copy.'

'But couldn't you tell me—'

'Tell you what? Don't you already know he was shot in the face at close range? Or would you rather I use some technical terms so you wouldn't understand a goddamn thing? And haven't I also told you that, although his thing was exposed, it hadn't been used?'

'Did you find the bullet?'

'Yes. And I sent it to Ballistics. It entered through the left eye-socket and tore his head apart.'

'Anything else?'

'Do you promise not to bug me for at least ten days if I tell you?'

'I swear.'

'Well, they didn't kill him right away.'

'What do you mean?'

'They stuck a big handkerchief or a white rag in his mouth to prevent him screaming. I found some filaments of white cloth wedged between his teeth. Sent them down to the lab. And after they'd shot him they pulled the cloth out of his mouth and took it with them.'

'Can I ask you a question?'

'If it's the last.'

'Why are you speaking in the plural? Do you think there was more than one killer?'

'Do you really want to know? To confuse you, my friend.'

He was a mean one, Pasquano, and enjoyed it.

But this business of the rag being crammed into Angelo's mouth was not something to be taken lightly.

It meant that the murder had not been committed on impulse. I came, I shot, I left. And goodnight.

No. Whoever went to see Angelo had some questions to ask him, wanted to know something from him. And needed some time to do this. That was why they'd put him in a state where he'd be forced to listen to what the other was saying or asking him, and would only take the rag out of his mouth when Angelo had decided to answer.

And maybe Angelo answered and was killed anyway. Or else he wouldn't or couldn't answer, and that was why he was killed. But why hadn't the killer left the rag in his mouth? Perhaps because he was hoping to lead the police down a less sure path? Or, more precisely, because he was trying to create a false lead by making it look like a crime of passion – a premise that, though supported by the bird outside the cage, would have been disproved if the rag had been found in the victim's mouth? Or was it because the rag wasn't a rag? Maybe it was a handkerchief with a monogram that might have led to the killer's first and last names?

He gave up and went out on to the veranda.

He sat down and looked dejectedly at the two pages Catarella had printed. He had never understood a damn thing about numbers. Back in school, he remembered, when his friends were already doing abscesses – no, wait: abscesses are something else, something you get in your mouth. So what were they called? Ah, yes. Abscissas. When his schoolmates were doing abscissas and coordinates, he was still having trouble with the multiplication table for the number 8.

On the first page there was a column of thirty-eight numbers on the left-hand side, which corresponded to a second column of thirty-eight numbers on the right-hand side.

On the second page, there were thirty-two numbers on the left, and thirty-two numbers on the right. Thus, the sum total of numbers on the left came to seventy, and there were seventy numbers on the right as well. Montalbano congratulated himself on this discovery, while having to admit to himself that the same conclusion could have been reached by a little kid in the third year.

Half an hour later, he made a discovery that gave him as much satisfaction as Marconi must surely have felt when he realized he'd invented the wireless telegraph or whatever it was. That is, he had discovered that the numbers in the left-hand columns were not all different but consisted of a group of fourteen numbers each repeated five times. The repetitions were not consecutive, but scattered as though at random within the two columns.

He took one of the two numbers in the left-hand column and copied it on to the back of one of the pages as many times as it was repeated. Next to it he wrote down the corresponding numbers from the right-hand column.

213452	*136000*
213452	*80000*
213452	*200000*
213452	*70000*
213452	*110000*

It seemed clear to him that while the number on the left was in code, the number on the right was in clear and referred to a sum of money. The total came to 596,000. Not much if it was in lire. But more than a billion lire if it was in euros, as was more likely. Thus the business dealings between Angelo and Signor 213452 came to that amount. Now, since there were another thirteen numbered gentlemen, and the corresponding numbers for each added up to about the same amount as those examined, this meant Angelo's business volume came to over twelve, thirteen billion lire, or six, six and a half million euros. To be kept, however, carefully hidden. Assuming everything conformed to his suppositions. It was not impossible that those figures meant something else.

His eyes started to fog, having trouble focusing on the numbers. He was getting tired. At this rate, he thought, it would take him three to five years to crack the code of the songs, and by the time it was all over he would surely be blind and walking around with a white stick or a dog in a harness.

He brought everything back inside, closed the door to the veranda, went out, got into his car and left. Since he was still a bit early for his appointment with Paola, he drove at less than ten miles per hour, driving everyone who happened to be behind him crazy. Every motorist, when they managed to pass him, felt obliged to insult him. Thus, he was a(n): faggot, according to a trucker; idiot, according to a priest; *cornuto*, according to a nice lady; ba-ba-ba-, according to a stutterer; but all these insults went in one ear and out the other. Only one made him angry. A distinguished-looking man of about sixty pulled up alongside him and said, 'Donkey!'

Donkey? How dared he? The inspector made a vain attempt to pursue the man, pressing down on the accelerator until he was at twenty miles an hour, but then preferred to slow down to his normal cruising speed.

Arriving at the Promenade, he couldn't find a parking space and had to drive around for a long time before he found a spot a long way from the appointed place. When he finally got there, Paola was already sitting at a table, waiting for him.

She ordered a Prosecco. Montalbano joined in.

'This morning, when Carlo heard there was a police inspector on the phone, he got a terrible fright.'

'I'm sorry, I didn't mean to—'

'Oh, that's just the way he is. He's a very sweet boy, but the mere sight of, say, a carabiniere driving beside him deeply upsets him. There's no explanation for it.'

'Maybe some research into his DNA could come up

with an explanation,' said Montalbano. 'He probably had a few ancestors who were outlaws. Ask him some time.'

They laughed. So the man who took up the school-teacher's free time on days when she didn't go to school was named Carlo. End of subject. They moved on to the matter at hand.

'Yesterday evening,' said Paola, 'when that business about Angelo dictating the letters to Elena came out, I felt really uncomfortable.'

'Why?'

'Because, despite Michela's opinion to the contrary, I think Elena was telling the truth.'

'How do you know?'

'You see, Inspector, during the time we were together, I wrote Angelo many letters. I used to like to write to him.'

'I didn't find any when I searched the apartment.'

'They were returned to me.'

'By Angelo?'

'No, by Michela. After her brother and I broke up. She didn't want them to end up in Elena's hands.'

Michela really couldn't stand Elena.

'You still haven't told me why you felt uncomfortable.'

'Well, one of those letters was dictated by Angelo.'

A big point for Elena! One that, moreover, could not be cast into doubt since it was scored by her defeated rival.

'Or, rather,' Paola continued, 'he gave me the general outlines. And since we broke up, I've never said anything to Michela about this little conspiracy.'

'You could have mentioned it last night.'

'Would you believe me if I said I didn't have the courage? Michela was so sure that Elena was lying.'

'Can you describe the contents of the letter?'

'Of course. Angelo had to go to Holland for a week, and Michela had made it clear she intended to go with him. So he got me to write a letter saying I'd asked for ten days' leave from school so I could accompany him. It wasn't true. It was exams time. Like they're going to give me a ten-day holiday during exams! Anyway, he said he'd show his sister the letter, and it would allow him to go alone, as he wished.'

'And if Michela had run into you in Montelusa when Angelo was in Holland, how would you have explained that to her?'

'Angelo and I had thought about this. I would have said that at the last moment the school withdrew permission.'

'And you didn't mind him going away alone?'

'Well, I did a little, of course. But I realized that it was important for Angelo to liberate himself for a few days from Michela's overbearing presence.'

'Overbearing?'

'I don't know how else to define it, Inspector. Words like "assiduous", "affectionate", "loving" don't really give a sense of it. They fall short. Michela felt this sort of absolute obligation to watch over her brother, as though he were a little boy.'

'What was she afraid of?'

'Nothing, I don't think. My explanation for it – there's nothing scientific about it, mind you, I don't know a thing about psychoanalysis. But in my opinion, it came from a sort of frustrated craving for motherhood that was transferred entirely, and apprehensively, to her brother.'

She gave her usual giggle.

'I've often thought that if I'd married Angelo, it would have been very hard for me to free myself not from my mother-in-law's clutches – since she, poor thing, counts for nothing – but from my sister-in-law's.'

She paused. Montalbano realized she was weighing the words she would use to express what she was thinking.

'When Angelo died, I expected Michela to fall apart. But the opposite happened.'

'Meaning?'

'She wailed, she screamed, she cried, yes, but at the same time I sensed a feeling of liberation in her at an unconscious level. It was as if she'd thrown off a weight. She seemed more serene, more free. You know what I mean?'

'Perfectly.'

Then, who knows why?, a question popped into his mind.

'Has Michela ever had a boyfriend?'

'Why do you ask?'

'Dunno, just wondering.'

'She told me that when she was nineteen she fell in love with a boy who was twenty-one. They were officially engaged for three years.'

'Why did they break up?'

'They didn't. He died. Apparently he was a very gifted motor cyclist but a little too fond of driving really fast. I don't know the details of the accident. After that, Michela never wanted to get close to men. And I think that from then on, she redoubled her vigilance over poor Angelo until she became asphyxiating.'

'You're an intelligent woman, you're in no way under investigation and you've long considered your relationship with Angelo over,' said Montalbano, looking her in the eye.

'Your preamble is a bit distressing,' said Paola, with her usual grin. 'What are you getting at?'

'I want an answer. Who was Angelo Pardo?'

She didn't seemed surprised by the question. 'I've asked myself the same thing, Inspector. And I don't mean when he left me for Elena. Because up till then I knew who Angelo was. He was an ambitious man, first of all.'

'I'd never thought of him in that light.'

'Because he didn't want to appear so. I think he suffered a lot from being expelled by the Medical Association. It cut short a very promising career. But, you see, even with the profession he had ... For example, within a year he would have had exclusive rights of representation for two multinational pharmaceutical companies across all of Sicily, not just Montelusa and its province.'

'He told you this?'

'No, but I overheard many of his phone conversations with Zurich and Amsterdam.'

'And when did you start asking yourself who Angelo Pardo was?'

'When he was killed. Things appear in a different light, things for which you had an explanation before and which now, after his death, are not so easily explained any more.'

'Such as?'

'Such as certain grey areas. He was capable of disappearing for a few days at a time and then, when he came back, he wouldn't tell you anything. You couldn't squeeze a single word out of him. In the end I was convinced he was seeing another woman, having some passing fling. But after the way he was killed, I'm no longer so sure he was having affairs.'

'What was he doing, then?'

Paola threw up her hands, disconsolate.

12

Before going to eat, Montalbano dropped in at the station. Catarella was sleeping in front of the computer, head thrown back, mouth open, saliva trickling down his chin. He did not wake up. The next phone call would take care of that.

On the inspector's desk was a dark blue canvas bag. A leather label stuck to the front bore the words 'Salmon House'. He opened it and realized it was insulated. Inside, there were five round, transparent plastic containers in which he could see large fillets of pickled herring swimming in multicoloured sauces. There also a whole smoked salmon. And an envelope wrapped in cellophane.

He opened it.

From Sweden with love. Ingrid.

Apparently she had found someone there from Sicily and taken the opportunity to send along that little gift. Suddenly he missed her so much that the desire to open one of those containers and have a little taste faded. When would she make up her mind to come back?

It was no longer possible to go to the trattoria. He had to race home and empty the bag into the refrigerator. Picking it up, he noticed there were three sheets of paper under it. The first was a note from Catarella.

Chief. Seeing as how I don't know weather or not your coming personally in person to the ofice, I'm leving you the printout of the siccond file which I had to stay up all nite to figger out the past word for but in the end I stuck it to that file I did.

The other two pages were all numbers. Two columns, as before. The left-hand figures were exactly the same as those in the first file. He pulled the pages he'd worked on that morning out of his jacket pocket and checked.

Identical. All that changed were the numbers in the second column. But he didn't feel like giving himself a headache.

He left the old pages, the new pages and the coded songbook on the desk, grabbed the canvas bag and went out of the room. Passing the cubby-hole at the entrance he heard Catarella yelling, 'No, sir, no, sir, I'm sorry but the inspector ain't in. This morning he said this morning he wasn't coming in this morning. Yessir, I'll tell 'im, certifiably. Have no fears, I'll tell 'im.'

'Was that for me, Cat?' asked the inspector, appearing before him.

Catarella looked at him as if he were Lazarus raised from the dead. '*Matre santa*, Chief, where djou come from?'

It was too complicated to explain that Catarella had been sleeping, drained after a night of battle with passwords, when Montalbano had come in. Never in a million years, moreover, would the diligent Catarella have admitted nodding off on the job at the switchboard.

'Who was it?' the inspector asked.

'Dr Latte wit' an S at the end. He said that seeing as how Mr C'mishner can't see you today, neither, the day we're at now, as you guys prearraigned, he says he rearraigned it for tomorrow, atta zack same time as was 'sposed to be on the day of today.'

'Cat, do you know you're brilliant?'

'For as how the way I 'splained what that Dr Latte wit' an S at the end said?'

'No, because you managed to open the second file.'

'Aaah, Chief! I straggled all night wit' it! You got no idea what kinda trouble I had! It was a past word that looked like one past word but rilly was—'

'Tell me about it later, Cat.'

He was afraid to waste time. The herrings and salmon in the bag might start to spoil.

But the moment he got home and opened the first container, the persuasive aroma invading his nostrils made him realize he needed to equip himself at once with a plate, a fork and a fresh loaf of bread.

At least half the contents of those containers needed

to go not into the refrigerator but straight into his belly. Only the salmon went into the fridge. After setting the table he took the rest outside on to the veranda.

The herrings, which were high-calibre, turned out to be marinated in a variety of preparations ranging from sweet-and-sour sauce to mustard. He had a feast. He really wanted to devour them, but realized he would spend the whole afternoon and evening wanting water, like someone stranded for days in the desert.

So he put what remained into the fridge and replaced his customary walk along the jetty with a long walk on the beach.

Then he took a shower and lolled about the house for a bit before returning to the station around four thirty. Catarella was not at his post. In compensation, he ran into a glum-faced Mimì Augello in the corridor. 'What's wrong, Mimì?'

'Where are you coming from? What are you doing?' Augello fired back edgily, following him into his office.

'*I come from Vigàta, and I'm doing my job as inspector,*' Montalbano crooned to the tune of 'Pale Little Lady'.

'Yeah, go ahead and play the wise guy. This is really not the time for that, Salvo.'

Montalbano got worried. 'Salvuccio's not well?'

'Salvuccio's great. It's me that's the problem, after a heavy dose of Liguori, who practically went nuts.'

'Why?'

'See? I was right to ask you where you've been! Don't you know what happened yesterday in Fanara?'

'No.'

'You didn't turn on your TV?'

'No. Come on, what happened?'

'MP di Cristoforo died.'

Di Cristoforo! Under-secretary for communications! Rising star of the ruling party, not to mention, according to gossips, a young man much admired in those circles where admiration goes hand in hand with staying alive.

'But he wasn't even fifty! What'd he die of?'

'Officially, a heart-attack. Owing to the stress of all the political commitments to which he so generously devoted himself ... and so on and so forth. Unofficially, from the same illness as Nicotra.'

'Fuck!'

'Exactly. Now you understand why Liguori, feeling the seat of his pants starting to burn, demands that we arrest the supplier before any more illustrious victims fall.'

'Listen, Mimì, weren't those gentlemen doing cocaine?'

'Of course.'

'But I'd always heard that coke wasn't—'

'That's what I thought, too. But Liguori, who's a first-class idiot but knows his trade well, explained to me that when coke isn't properly cut, or is cut with certain other substances, it can turn poisonous. And both Nicotra and di Cristoforo died of poisoning.'

'But I don't get it, Mimì. What interest could a dealer have in killing his clients?'

'Well, it wasn't intentional. It's just a bit of collateral damage. According to Liguori, our dealer didn't only deal. He also further cut the merchandise, by himself and with inadequate means, doubling the quantity before putting it on the market.'

'So there might be other deaths.'

'Absolutely.'

'And what's lighting a fire under us all is that this dealer supplies a high-flying circle of politicians, businessmen, established professionals and so on.'

'You said it.'

'But how did Liguori come to the conclusion that the dealer is in Vigàta?'

'He merely hinted that he'd deduced it from clues provided by an informer.'

'Best wishes, Mimì.'

'What do you mean, "best wishes"? Is that all you have to say?'

'Mimì, I told you yesterday what I had to say. Make your moves very carefully. This is not a police operation.'

'Isn't it? Then what is it?'

'It's a secret-service operation, Mimì. For the guys who work in the shadows and are followers of Stalin.'

Mimì frowned.

'What's Stalin got to do with this?'

'Apparently Uncle Joe once said that when a man becomes a problem, you need only eliminate the man to eliminate the problem.'

'What's that got to do with this?'

'I've already told you, and I repeat: the only solution is to kill this dealer, or have him killed. Think about it. Let's say you go by the book and arrest him. When you're writing the report, you can't very well say he's responsible for the deaths of Nicotra and di Cristoforo.'

'Can't I?'

'No, you can't. Mimì, you're more thick-headed than a Calabrian. Senator Nicotra and MP di Cristoforo were respectable, honourable men, paragons of virtue – all church, family, public service. No drugs, of any sort, ever. If need be, ten thousand witnesses will testify in their favour. So, you weigh the pros and cons and come to the conclusion that it's better to gloss over this business of their deaths. And you end up writing that the guy's a dealer, and that's all. But what if the guy starts talking to the prosecutor? What if he blurts out the names of Nicotra and di Cristoforo?'

'Nobody would voluntarily incriminate himself in two homicides, even unintentional ones! What are you saying?'

'OK, let's say he doesn't incriminate himself. There's still the risk that someone else might link the dealer to the two deaths. Don't forget, Mimì, Nicotra and di Cristoforo were politicians with many enemies. And in our neck of the woods, and not only our neck of the woods, politics is the art of burying one's adversary in shit.'

'What's politics got to do with me?'

'A lot, even if you don't realize it. In a case like this, do you know what your role is?'

'No. What is it?'

'You supply the shit.'

'That sounds a little excessive.'

'Excessive? Once it comes out that Nicotra and di Cristoforo used drugs and died from it, their memory will be unanimously dumped on in direct proportion to the equally unanimous praise that will be heaped on you for having arrested the dealer. Some three months later, at most, somebody from Nicotra and di Cristoforo's party will start by revealing that Nicotra took very small doses of drugs for medicinal purposes, and that di Cristoforo did the same for his ingrown toenail. We're talking medicine here, not vice. Then, little by little, their memory will be rehabilitated, and people will start saying that it was you who first slung mud at the dear departed.'

'Me?'

'Yes, you, by making a careless arrest, to say the least.'

Augello stood there, speechless.

Montalbano threw down his ace. 'Don't you see what's happening to the "Clean Hands" judges? They're being blamed for the suicides and heart-attacks of some of the accused. The fact that the accused were corrupt and corrupters and deserved to go to jail gets glossed over. According to these sensitive souls, the real culprit is not the culprit who in a moment of shame commits suicide but the judge who made him feel ashamed. Anyway, we've talked enough about this. If you get it, you get it. If you don't, I'm tired of explaining it to you. Now get out of here, I've got work to do.'

Without a word, Mimì got up and left the room, even glummer than before. Montalbano started eyeing four pages densely covered with numbers, unable to make anything whatsoever of them.

After five minutes of this, he pushed them away in disgust and rang the switchboard. A voice he didn't recognize answered.

'Listen, I want you to find me the phone number of a Palermo contractor named Mario Sciacca.'

'Home or business phone?'

'Home.'

'All right.'

'But just find me the number, understand? If the home phone's not listed, ask our colleagues in Palermo. Then I'll call from a direct line.'

'I understand, Inspector. You don't want them to know it's the police.'

Smart kid. Knew his stuff.

'What's the name?'

'Sciacca, Inspector.'

'No, yours.'

'Amato, Inspector. I started working here a month ago.'

He made a mental note to talk to Fazio about this Amato. The kid might be worth having on the squad. A few minutes later the phone rang. Amato had found Mario Sciacca's home phone number.

The inspector dialled it.

'Who's this?' asked an old woman's voice.

'Is that the Sciacca residence?'

'Yes.'

'My name is Antonio Volpe. I'd like to speak with Signora Teresa.'

'My daughter-in-law's not in.'

'Is she away?'

'Well, she's gone to Montelusa. Her father's sick.'

What a stroke of luck! This might spare him the boring drive to Palermo. He looked for the number in the phone book. There were four people named Cacciatore. He would have to be patient and try them all.

'The Cacciatore residence?'

'No, the Mistrettas'. Look, this whole thing is a big pain in the arse,' said an angry male voice.

'What whole thing, if I may ask?'

'The fact that you all keep calling when the Cacciatores moved away a year ago.'

'Do you know their number, by any chance?'

Mr Mistretta hung up without answering. A fine start,

no doubt about it. Montalbano dialled the second number. 'The Cacciatore residence?'

'Yes,' replied a pleasant female voice.

'Signora, my name is Antonio Volpe. I tried to get in touch with a certain Teresa Sciacca in Palermo, and was told—'

'I'm Teresa Sciacca.'

Astonished by his sudden good fortune, Montalbano was speechless.

'Hello?' said Teresa.

'How's your father? I was told that—'

'He's much better, thank you. So much better that I'll be going back to Palermo tomorrow.'

'I absolutely must speak to you before you leave.'

'Signor Volpe, I—'

'Actually my name's not Volpe. I'm Inspector Montalbano.'

Teresa Sciacca let out a kind of gasp between fright and surprise. 'Oh, my God! Has something happened to Mario?'

'Don't worry, Signora, your husband's fine. I need to talk to you about something involving you.'

A very long pause. Then a 'Yes' that was a sigh, a breath.

'Believe me, I would have preferred not to stir up unpleasant memories, but—'

'I understand.'

'I guarantee that our meeting will remain confidential, and I give you my word never to mention your name in the investigation, for any reason whatsoever.'

'I don't see how I could be of use to you. It's been so many years since ... In any case, you can't come here.'

'Could you come out?'

'Yes, I could leave for about an hour.'

'Tell me where you want to meet.'

Teresa gave him the name of a café in the elevated part of Montelusa. Five thirty. The inspector glanced at his watch. He had barely enough time to get into his car and go. To arrive in time, he would have to drive at the insane speed of forty to forty-five miles per hour.

*

Teresa Sciacca *née* Cacciatore was a thirty-eight-year-old woman who looked like a good mother, and it was immediately clear that this look was not facade but substance. She was quite embarrassed by their meeting, and Montalbano immediately came to her aid. 'Signora, in ten minutes, at the most, you'll be able to go home.'

'Thank you, but I really don't see how what happened twenty years ago could have anything to do with Angelo's death.'

'It has nothing to do with it. But it's essential for me to understand certain modes of behaviour. Understand?'

'No, but go ahead and ask your questions.'

'How did Angelo react when you told him you were expecting?'

'He was happy, and we immediately talked about getting married. In fact, I started looking for a house the very next day.'

'Did your family know?'

'They didn't know anything. They didn't even know Angelo. Then one evening he told me he'd changed his mind. He said it was crazy to get married, that it would ruin his career – he showed a lot of promise as a doctor, that was true. And so he started talking about abortion.'

'And what did you do?'

'I took it badly. We had a terrible row. When we finally calmed down, I told him I was going to tell my parents everything. He got really scared. Papa's not a man to mess with, and he begged me not to. I gave him three days.'

'To do what?'

'To think about it. He phoned me on the second, in the afternoon. It was a Wednesday. I remember it well. He asked if we could meet. When I got there, he immediately told me he'd found a solution and needed my help. His solution was this: the following Sunday, he and I would go to my parents and tell them everything. Then Angelo would explain to them why he couldn't marry me straight away. He needed at least two years without any ties. A famous doctor wanted him for an assistant, which meant he would have to live abroad for eighteen months. In short, after giving birth, I would live at home with my parents until Angelo had set himself up here. He even said he was ready to acknowledge paternity of the child, to set my parents' minds at rest. And then, in short, he would marry me in about two years' time.'

'How did you take this?'

'It seemed like a good solution to me. And I told him so. I had no reason to doubt his sincerity. So he suggested we celebrate, and he even invited Michela, his sister.'

'Had you already met?'

'Yes, we'd even got together a few times, though she didn't seem to like me very much. Anyway, we were all supposed to meet at nine p.m. in the surgery of a colleague of Angelo's, after visiting hours.'

'Why not at his own surgery?'

'Because he didn't have one. He worked out of a little room this colleague let him use. When I got there the colleague had already left, and Michela hadn't arrived. Angelo gave me a glass of bitter orange soda. As soon as I'd drunk it, everything turned foggy and confused. I couldn't move or react ... I remember Angelo putting on his white coat, and ...'

She tried to go on, but Montalbano interrupted her. 'I get the picture. No need to continue.' He fired up a cigarette. Teresa wiped her eyes with a handkerchief.

'What do you remember after that?'

'My memory is still cloudy. Michela in a white uniform,

like a nurse, Angelo saying something … Then I'm in Angelo's car, I remember … then at Anna's place … She's a cousin of mine who knows everything … I spent the night there … Anna had called my parents and told them I'd be sleeping over … The next day I had a terrible haemorrhage and was rushed to hospital and had to tell Papa everything. And Papa pressed charges against Angelo.'

'So you never saw Angelo's colleague?'

'Never.'

'Thank you, Signora. That'll be all,' said Montalbano, standing up.

She looked surprised and relieved. She held out her hand to say goodbye. But instead of shaking it, the inspector kissed it.

13

He arrived a bit early for his appointment with Marshal
Laganà.

'You're looking good,' said the marshal, eyeing him.

Montalbano got worried. Often, in recent times, that
statement hadn't sounded right to him. If someone tells
you you're looking good, it means they were expecting
you not to look so good. And why were they thinking this? Because you've reached an age at which the
worst could happen overnight. To take one example: up
to a certain point in life, if you slip and fall, you get
up straight away because nothing's happened to you.
Then the moment comes when you slip and fall and
you can't get up because you've broken your femur.
What's happened? What's happened is, you've crossed
the invisible boundary between one stage of life and the
next.

'You're looking good yourself,' the inspector lied,
with a certain satisfaction.

To his eyes, Laganà had aged quite a bit since the last time he'd seen him.

'I'm at your service,' said the marshal.

Montalbano filled him in on the murder of Angelo Pardo. And told him how Nicolò Zito, the reporter, when speaking to him in private, had led him to suspect that the motive for the killing could perhaps be found in the work that Pardo had been doing. He was beating around the bush, but Laganà understood at once and interrupted, 'Kickbacks?'

'It's a possible hypothesis,' the inspector said cautiously. And he told him about the gifts beyond his means that Pardo had given to his girlfriend, the missing strongbox, the secret bank account Montalbano hadn't been able to locate. In the end he pulled out of his jacket pocket the four computer printouts and coded songbook, then laid them on Laganà's desk.

'You can't say this gentleman was very fond of transparency,' the marshal commented, after examining these materials.

'Can you help me?' asked Montalbano.

'Certainly,' said the marshal, 'but don't expect something overnight. And before I begin I'll need some basic but essential information. What firms was he working for? And what doctors and pharmacies was he in contact with?'

'I've got a big diary of Pardo's in the car that should have most of the things you're looking for.'

Laganà gave him a confused look. 'Why did you leave it in the car?'

'I wanted first to make sure you were interested in the case. I'll go and get it.'

'Yes, and in the meantime I'll photocopy these pages and the songbook.'

✻

Therefore – the inspector recapitulated while driving back to Vigàta – Signora (pardon, Signorina) Michela Pardo had only told him half the story concerning the abortion performed on Teresa Cacciatore, completely leaving out her own major role. For Teresa it must have been like a scene from a horror film: first the deception and the trap, then, in crescendo, her boyfriend turning into her torturer and poking around inside her while she lay naked on the examination table unable even to open her mouth; then her future sister-in-law in a white uniform, preparing the instruments . . .

What sort of complicity had there been between Angelo and Michela? Out of what twisted instinct of sibling attachment had it arisen and solidified? How far had they taken their bond? And, given all this, what else were they capable of?

Then again, on second thoughts, what had any of this to do with the investigation? From Teresa's words – and there was no doubt she was telling the truth – it had become clear that Angelo was a rascal, which Montalbano had been thinking for some time, and that his dear sister wouldn't have hesitated to commit murder just to please her dear brother, which Montalbano had also been thinking for some time. What Teresa had told him confirmed what the brother and sister were like, but it didn't move the investigation a single inch forward.

✢

'Aah, Chief, Chief!' Catarella yelled from his cubby-hole. 'I got some importance to tell ya!'

'Did you beat the last last word?'

'Not yet, Chief. Iss complix. What I wannet a say is 'at Dacter Arquaraquà called.'

What was going on? The chief of Forensics had telephoned him? *The tombs shall open, the dead shall rise ...*

'Arquà, Cat, his name's Arquà.'

'His name's whatever 'is name is, Chief, you got the pitcher anyways.'

'What did he want?'

'He didn't say, Chief. But he axed me to ax you to call him when you got back.'

'Fazio here?'

'I tink so.'

'Go and find him and tell him to come to my office.'

While waiting, he called the lab in Montelusa. 'Arquà, were you looking for me?'

The two men didn't like each other, and so, by mutual, tacit agreement, they dispensed with greetings whenever they spoke.

'I suppose you already know that Dr Pasquano found two threads stuck between Angelo Pardo's teeth.'

'Yes.'

'We've analysed them and identified the fabric. It's Crilicon.'

'Does that come from Krypton?' It was a stupid quip that just slipped out of him.

Arquà, who obviously didn't read comic strips and didn't know of the existence of Superman, balked. 'What did you say?'

'Nothing, never mind. Why does that fabric seem important to you?'

'Because it's very particular and is mainly used for a specific article of clothing.'

'Namely?'

'Women's panties.'

Arquà hung up, and Montalbano sat there flummoxed, receiver in hand.

Another *noir* film? As he set the phone down, he imagined the scene.

TERRACE WITH ROOM.

Outside/inside shot, night.

Through the open door, from outside on the terrace,

the camera frames the interior of the former laundry room. Angelo is sitting on the arm of the armchair. The woman, standing in front of him and seen from behind, puts her handbag on the table and, very slowly, removes first her blouse, then her bra. The camera zooms entirely inside.

Sensual music.

With desire in his eyes, Angelo watches the woman unfasten her skirt, letting it drop to her feet. Angelo slides off the arm and into the chair, almost lying down.

The woman takes off her panties, but keeps them in her hand.

Angelo opens the zipper on his jeans and gets ready to have sex.

Extremely sensual music.

The woman opens her handbag and extracts something we can't see. Then she straddles Angelo, who embraces her.

Long, passionate kiss. Angelo's hands caress the woman's back. She suddenly breaks free of his embrace and points the pistol she has taken out of her handbag at Angelo's face.

Close-up of Angelo, terrified.

ANGELO   What ... what are you doing?
WOMAN   Open your mouth.

Angelo automatically obeys. The woman sticks the panties into his mouth. He tries to scream but can't.

WOMAN   Now I'm going to ask you a question. If you want to answer, just nod and I'll take them out of your mouth.

The camera follows her movements as she leans forward. She whispers something in his ear. His eyes open wide as he starts desperately shaking his head, 'No.'

Dramatic music.

WOMAN   I'll repeat my question.

She leans forward again, brings her mouth to Angelo's ear. Her lips move.

Close-up of Angelo still refusing, in the throes of uncontrollable panic.

WOMAN   As you wish.

She gets up, takes a step back, and shoots Angelo in the face.

Extreme close-up of Angelo's devastated head, a black, bloody hole where his eye used to be.

Tragic music.

Detail of Angelo's half-open mouth. Two tapered fingers reach into it and extract the panties. To put them on, the woman turns towards the camera, but the frame is shot from an angle that keeps her face hidden. She continues getting dressed, without any hurry. There's no trace of nervousness in her gestures.

Extreme close-up of Angelo's head, a horrendous sight.

Slow fade-out.

Granted, a dreadful script from a B-movie of the erotic-crime genre. It might, however, have had decent success on television, among all the other crap that gets broadcast. You know, TV movies. The inspector consoled himself with the thought that if he had to leave the police force he could try his hand at this new profession.

Leaving his private cinema to return to his office, he saw Fazio standing in front of his desk, staring at him inquisitively. 'What were you thinking, Chief?'

'Nothing, I was just watching a film. What do you want?'

'Chief, you're the one who called me.'

'Ah, yes. Have a seat. Got any news for me?'

'You said you wanted to know everything I could find out about Emilio Sclafani and Angelo Pardo. As for the schoolmaster, I have a little detail to add to what I already told you.'

'What's this little detail?'

'Remember how the schoolmaster sent his wife's lover to hospital?'

'Yes.'

'Well, he, too, was sent to hospital.'

'By whom?'

'A jealous husband.'

'That's not possible. The guy can't—'

'Chief, I assure you it's true. It happened before his second marriage.'

'He was caught in bed with the man's wife?' He couldn't accept that Elena had told him a lie – a lie so big it cast everything into doubt.

'No, Chief. It's got nothing to do with the bed. The schoolmaster lived in a great big apartment building and two of his windows gave on to the courtyard. You remember that movie . . .'

Another film? This wasn't an investigation any more, it was one of the countless film festivals!

'. . . the one about a photographer with a broken leg who spends his time looking out of his window across a courtyard and finds out some lady's been killed?'

'Yes. *Rear Window*, by Hitchcock.'

'Well, the schoolmaster bought himself a powerful set of binoculars, but he only watched the window across from his, where a young bride of about twenty lived, and since she didn't know she was being watched, she walked around her apartment half naked. Then one day the husband got wise to the schoolmaster's tricks, went over to his place and busted his head and his binoculars.'

Montalbano became almost certain that Sclafani had

demanded his wife give him a detailed report of what she did at each of her encounters with her lover. Why hadn't Elena told him this? Was it, perhaps, because this little detail (and what a detail!) cast the schoolmaster in a different light from that of the understanding, impotent husband and brought to the surface all the murk deep down in his soul?

'And what can you tell me about Angelo Pardo?'

'Nothing.'

'What do you mean, nothing?'

'Chief, nobody had the slightest thing to say against him. As far as the present was concerned, he earned a good living as a pharmaceutical representative, enjoyed life, and had no enemies.'

Montalbano knew Fazio too well to let slide what he'd just said – that is: 'as far as the present was concerned'.

'And as far as the past is concerned?'

Fazio smiled at him, and the inspector smiled back. They understood each other at once.

'There are two things in his past. One of these you already know, and it involves that business about the abortion.'

'Forget it, I already know all about it.'

'The other thing goes even further back – to the death of Angelo's sister's boyfriend.'

Montalbano felt a kind of jolt run down his spine. His ears pricked.

'The boyfriend was named Roberto Anzalone,' said Fazio. 'An engineering student who liked to race motorcycles as a hobby. That's why the accident that killed him seemed odd.'

'Why?'

'My dear Inspector, does it seem normal to you that such a skilled motorcyclist, after a two-mile straight, would ignore a bend and keep going, straight off a three-hundred-foot cliff?'

'Mechanical failure?'

'The motorbike was so smashed up after the accident, the experts couldn't make head or tail of it.'

'What about the post-mortem?'

'That's the best part. When he had the accident, Anzalone had just finished eating at a trattoria with a friend. The post-mortem showed he'd probably over-indulged in alcohol or something similar.'

'What's that supposed to mean, "something similar"? It was either alcohol or it wasn't.'

'Chief, the person who did the post-mortem was unable to specify. He simply wrote he found something similar to alcohol.'

'Bah. Go on.'

'The only problem is that the Anzalone family, when they found this out, said that Roberto didn't drink and demanded a new post-mortem. Most importantly, the waiter at the trattoria also stated that he hadn't served wine or any other kind of alcohol at that table.'

'Did they get the second post-mortem?'

'They did, but they had to wait three months for it. And, actually, given all the authorizations that were needed, that was pretty fast. The fact is that this time the alcohol, or whatever it was, wasn't there any more. And so the case was closed.'

'Tell me something. Do you know who the friend was who ate with him?'

Fazio's eyes started to sparkle. This happened whenever he knew that his words would have a dramatic effect. He was foretasting his pleasure.

'It was——' he began.

But Montalbano, who could be a real bastard when he wanted to, decided to spoil the effect for him. 'That's enough, I already know,' he said.

'How did you find out?' asked Fazio, between disappointment and wonder.

'Your eyes told me,' said the inspector. 'It was his future brother-in-law, Angelo Pardo. Was he interrogated?'

'Of course. And he confirmed the waiter's statement that they hadn't drunk wine or any other alcoholic beverage at the table. In any case, for some reason or other, Angelo Pardo had his lawyer present every time he made his three depositions. And his lawyer was none other than Senator Nicotra.'

'Nicotra!' marvelled the inspector. 'That's much too big a fish for a testimony of so little importance.'

Fazio never found out whether, in uttering Nicotra's name, he'd actually managed to get even for the disappointment of a moment before. But if anyone had asked Montalbano why he'd reacted so strongly to the news that Nicotra and Angelo had known one another for quite some time, he would not have known what to answer.

'But where would Angelo have found the money to inconvenience a lawyer of Senator Nicotra's stature?'

'It didn't cost him a penny, Chief. Angelo's father had been a campaigner for the senator, and they'd become friends. Their families spent time together. In fact, the senator also represented Angelo when he was accused of the abortion.'

'Anything else?'

'Yes, sir.'

'You going to tell me free of charge or do I have to pay for it?' asked Montalbano, when he saw that Fazio couldn't make up his mind to go on.

'No, Chief, it's all included in my salary.'

'Then out with it.'

'It's something that was told me by only one person. I haven't been able to confirm it.'

'Just tell me, for what it's worth.'

'Apparently a year ago Angelo got into the bad habit of gambling and often lost.'

'A lot?'

'Lots and lots.'

'Could you be more precise?'

'Tens of millions of lire.'

'Was he in debt?'

'Apparently not.'

'Where did he gamble?'

'At some den in Fanara.'

'You know anyone around there?'

'In Fanara? No, Chief.'

'Shame.'

'Why?'

'Because I'd bet my family jewels that Angelo had another bank account other than the one we already know about. Since it seems he didn't have any debts, where was he getting the money he lost? Or to pay for the gifts to his girlfriend? After what you've just told me, I think this mysterious bank may very well be in Fanara. See what you can come up with there.'

'I'll try.'

Fazio stood up. When he was at the door, Montalbano said softly, 'Thanks.'

Fazio stopped, turned and looked at him. 'For what? It's all included in my salary, Chief.'

*

The inspector hurried back to Marinella. The salmon Ingrid had sent him was anxiously awaiting him.

14

It was pouring. With him getting drenched, cursing, blaspheming, the water running down his hair, into his collar, then sliding down his back, triggering cold shudders, his sodden socks now filtering the water flowing into his shoes, the door to his house in Marinella wouldn't open because the keys wouldn't go into the lock, and when they did they wouldn't turn. He tried four different keys, one after the other, but it was hopeless. How could he go on like this, getting soaked to the bone, unable to set foot in his own house?

Finally he decided to have a look at the keys in his hand. To his shock, he realized they weren't his. He must mistakenly have grabbed someone else's, but where?

Then he remembered that the mistake might have happened in Boccadasse, at a bar where they made good coffee. But he'd been in Boccadasse two weeks ago! How could he have been back in Vigàta for two weeks without ever going into his house?

'Where are my keys?' he shouted.

It seemed that no one could hear him, so loudly was the rain drumming on the roof, on his head, on the ground, on the leaves in the trees. Then he thought he heard a woman's voice far, far away, coming and going with the intensity of the downpour.

'Turn the corner! Turn the corner!' said the voice.

What did it mean? Whatever the case, lost as he was, he took four steps and turned the corner. He found himself in Michela's bathroom. The woman was naked and dipped her hand into the bathwater to feel the temperature. In so doing she offered him a remarkably hilly panorama on which the eye willingly lingered.

'Come on, get in.'

He realized he was also naked, but this did not surprise him. He got into the bath and lay down. It was a good thing he was immediately covered with soapsuds. He felt embarrassed that Michela might see the semi-erection he'd got on contact with the warm water.

'I'll fetch your keys and the present,' said Michela.

She went out. What present was she talking about? Was it his birthday, perhaps? But when was he born? He'd forgotten. He stopped asking himself questions, closed his eyes and abandoned himself to the relief he was feeling. Later, when he heard her return, he opened his eyes to little slits. But then they popped wide, for in the bathroom doorway stood not Michela but Angelo, his face ravaged by the gunshot, blood still running down his shirt, the zipper of his jeans open and his thingy hanging out, a revolver in his hand, pointed at him.

'What do you want?' he asked, frightened.

The bathwater had suddenly turned ice cold. With his left hand Angelo gestured for him to wait, then brought his hand to his mouth and pulled out a pair of panties. He took two steps forward. 'Open your mouth!' he ordered.

Clenching his teeth, Montalbano shook his head. Never in a million years would he let him stick those panties in his mouth. They were still wet with the spittle of that entity who, being a corpse, had no right, logically speaking, to be threatening him with a gun. Or even to walk, if one really thought about it. Although, all things considered, he still looked pretty well preserved, given that it had been many days since the murder. Whatever the case, it was clear that the inspector now found himself in a trap laid by Michela to abet her brother in some shady affair of his.

'Are you going to open up or not?'

He shook his head again and the other man fired. A deafening blast.

Montalbano jolted awake and sat up in bed, heart racing at a gallop, body covered with sweat. The shutter, blown by the wind, had slammed against the wall, and outside a storm had indeed broken out.

It was five o'clock in the morning. By nature the inspector didn't believe in premonitions, forebodings or anything to do with paranormal phenomena in general. Normality itself seemed already sufficiently abnormal to him. There was, however, one thing he was convinced of: that sometimes his dreams were nothing other than the paradoxical or fantastical elaborations of a line of reasoning he'd begun to follow in his head before falling asleep. And as for the interpretation of those dreams, he had more faith in the self-appointed interpreters of Lotto numbers than in Sigmund Freud.

So, what did that muddle of a dream mean?

After half an hour of turning it over and over in his head, he managed to isolate two elements that seemed important.

The first concerned Angelo's keys. The first set had been in his possession since the crime lab had returned them to him. The other set, the one he'd asked Michela to give him, he'd handed back to her. All of this seemed normal, yet something about those keys had set his brain going, something that didn't add up and which he couldn't bring into focus. He would have to give this more thought later.

The other element was a word, 'present', that Michela had said to him before leaving the bathroom. When Michela had actually spoken to him about presents, however, it had always been in reference to the expensive gifts Angelo had made to Elena...

Stop right there, Montalbà. You're getting warm, warmer, warmer, hot, hot! You're there! Shit, you're there!

He felt such immense satisfaction that he grabbed the alarm clock, pushed down the button that turned off the ring, laid his head on the pillow and fell immediately asleep.

*

Elena opened the door. She was barefoot and wearing the dangerous half-length housecoat she'd had on the previous time, face still dotted with a few drops of water from the shower she'd just had. It was ten o'clock in the morning, and she must have woken up not long before that. She smelled so strongly of young, fresh skin that it seemed unbearable to the inspector. Upon seeing him she smiled, took his hand and, still holding it, pulled him inside. She closed the door and led him into the living room.

'The coffee's ready,' she said.

Montalbano had barely sat down when she reappeared with the tray. They drank their coffee without speaking.

'You want to know something strange, Inspector?' asked Elena, setting down her empty cup.

'Tell me.'

'A little while ago, when you phoned to tell me you were coming, I felt happy. I'd missed you.'

Montalbano's heart did exactly what an aeroplane does when it hits an air pocket. But he said nothing, pretended to be concentrating on his last sip of coffee, and set his cup down as well.

'Any news?' she asked.

'A little,' the inspector said cautiously.

'I, on the other hand, have none,' said Elena.

Montalbano made an inquisitive face. He didn't understand the meaning of those words.

Elena laughed heartily. 'What a funny face you just made! I meant that for the last two days Emilio hasn't stopped asking me if there's any news, and I keep saying, "No, there's no news."'

Montalbano was not convinced. Elena's explanation only confused matters; it didn't clarify them. 'I didn't know your husband was so interested in the case.'

Elena laughed even harder.

'He's not. He's interested in me.'

'I don't understand.'

'Inspector, Emilio wants to know if I've already taken measures to replace Angelo, or if I'm intending to do so at any time soon.'

So that was what this was all about! The old pig was apparently in crisis with no lewd stories being told to him by his wife. Montalbano decided to give her a little rope. 'Why haven't you?'

He was expecting her to laugh again, but Elena turned serious. 'I don't want there to be any misunderstandings, and I want to feel at peace. I'm waiting for the investigation to be over.' She smiled again. 'So you should hurry up.'

And why would a new relationship with another man

create misunderstandings? He got the answer to his question when his gaze met hers. This wasn't a woman sitting in the armchair in front of him but a cheetah at rest, still sated. The moment she began to feel the pangs of hunger, however, she would pounce on the prey she had already long singled out. And that prey was him, Inspector Salvo Montalbano, a trembling, clumsy little domestic animal who would never manage to outrun those extremely long, springy legs, which for the moment were deceptively crossed. And, most troubling of all, once those fangs sank into his flesh and that tongue began to savour him, he would quickly prove bland to the cheetah's tastes and disappointing to the schoolmaster husband in the story that the cheetah was certain to tell him. His only hope was to play the fool to avoid going to war, and pretend not to have understood.

'I came today for two reasons.'

'You could have come anyway, for no reason at all.'

The beast had her eye on him, and there was no distracting her.

'You told me that, aside from the car, Angelo had given you jewellery.'

'Yes. Would you like to see it?'

'No, I'm not interested in seeing it. I'm more interested in the boxes the jewels came in. Do you still have them?'

'Yes.'

She got up, picked up the tray and took it away. She returned at once and handed the inspector two black boxes, already open and empty. They were lined with white silk and each bore the same inscription: *A. Dimora Jewellery – Montelusa.*

This was what he wanted to know and what his dream had suggested to him. He gave the boxes back to Elena, who put them on the coffee-table.

'And what was the other reason?' she asked.

'That's harder to say. The post-mortem revealed an important detail. Two threads were found stuck between the victim's teeth. The crime lab informed me that they were from a special fabric used almost exclusively in the manufacture of women's panties.'

'What does that mean?' asked Elena.

'It means that someone, before shooting him, stuck a pair of panties into his mouth to stop him screaming. Add to this that the victim was found in a state suggesting he'd been about to engage in a sexual act. It being rather inconceivable that a man would go around with a pair of women's panties in his pocket, it therefore means the person who killed him was not a man but a woman.'

'I see,' said Elena. 'A crime of passion, apparently.'

'Exactly. At this point in the investigation, however, it's my duty to report all my findings to the prosecutor.'

'So you'll have to mention me.'

'Of course. And Prosecutor Tommaseo will immediately

call you in for questioning. The death threats you made to Angelo in your letters will be seen as evidence against you.'

'What should I do?'

Montalbano's admiration for the girl increased a few notches. She hadn't become afraid or agitated. She had asked for information, nothing more. 'Find a good lawyer.'

'Can I tell him that it was Angelo who made me write those letters?'

'Certainly. And when you do, tell him he should ask Paola Torrisi a few questions.'

Elena wrinkled her brow. 'Angelo's ex? Why?'

Montalbano threw up his hands. He couldn't tell her. That would be saying too much. But the mechanism in Elena's head worked better than that of a Swiss watch. 'Did he also get her to write letters like mine?'

Montalbano threw up his hands again. 'The problem is that you, Elena, haven't got an alibi for the night of the crime. You told me you drove around for a few hours and therefore didn't meet anyone. However ...'

'However?'

'I don't believe you.'

'Do you think I killed Angelo?'

'I don't believe you didn't meet anyone that evening. I'm convinced you could produce an alibi if you wanted to, but you don't.'

She looked at him, eyes popping. 'How ... how do you ...'

Now she was agitated indeed. The inspector felt pleased he had hit the mark. 'The last time I asked you if you'd met anyone during the time you were wandering about in your car, you said no. But before speaking, you sort of hesitated. That was the first and last time you hesitated. And I realized you didn't want to tell me the truth. But be careful: not having an alibi might lead to your arrest.'

Suddenly she turned pale. One must strike while the iron's hot, Montalbano told himself, hating himself for the cliché and for playing the tormentor.

'You're going to have to be escorted to the station ...'

It wasn't true. That wasn't the procedure, but those were the magic words. And indeed Elena began to tremble, a veil of sweat appearing on her brow. 'I haven't told Emilio and I didn't want him to know.'

What had her husband to do with this? Was the schoolmaster fated to pop up everywhere, like Pierino, the famous puppet, in the story his mother used to tell him as a child? 'What didn't you want him to know?'

'That I was with a man that evening.'

'Who was it?'

'A filling-station attendant ... It's the only station on the road to Giardina. His name is Luigi. I don't know his last name. I stopped to get petrol. He was closing, but he reopened for me. He started flirting, and I didn't say no. I wanted ... I wanted to forget Angelo forever.'

'How long were you together?'

'A couple of hours.'

'Could he testify to that?'

'I don't think it would be a problem. He's very young, about twenty, unmarried.'

'Tell that to the lawyer. Maybe he can find a way to keep your husband from getting wind of it.'

'I would be very unhappy if he found out. I betrayed his trust.'

But how did this husband and wife reason? He felt at sea. Then Elena was suddenly laughing again, hard, her head thrown backwards.

'Let me in on the joke.'

'A woman supposedly stuck her panties in Angelo's mouth so he couldn't scream?'

'So it seems.'

'I'm only telling you because it couldn't have been me.' She had another laughing fit that almost brought tears to her eyes.

'Come on, out with it.'

'Because whenever I knew I was going to see Angelo I didn't wear panties. Anyway, do these look like they could be used to gag anyone?'

She stood up, hiked up her bathrobe, spun round in a circle and sat down again. She'd performed the movement perfectly naturally, without modesty or immodesty. Her panties were smaller than a G-string. With those in his mouth, a man could still have recited all of Cicero's *Catinarian Orations* or sung 'Celeste Aïda'.

'I have to go,' said the inspector, standing up.

He absolutely had to get away from the woman. Alarm bells and warning lights were going off wildly in his head. Elena also stood up, and approached him. Unable to keep her away with his extended arms, he stopped her with words. 'One last thing.'

'What is it?'

'We've learned that Angelo had recently been gambling and losing a lot of money.'

'*Really?*'

She seemed truly puzzled.

'So you know nothing about it.'

'I never even suspected it. Did he gamble here, in Vigàta?'

'No. In Fanara, apparently. At a clandestine gambling den. Did you ever go with him to Fanara?'

'Yes, once. But we came back to Vigàta the same evening.'

'Can you remember if Angelo went into any banks that day in Fanara?'

'Out of the question. He made me wait in the car outside three doctors' surgeries and two pharmacies. I nearly died of boredom. Oh, but I do remember –

because I heard about him on TV after he died – that we also stopped outside the villa of di Cristoforo, the Member of Parliament.'

'Did he *know* him?'

'Apparently.'

'How long did he stay inside the villa?'

'Just a few minutes.'

'Did he say why he went there?'

'No, and I didn't ask. I'm sorry.'

'Another question, but this really will be the last.'

'Ask me as many as you like.'

'Did Angelo do coke, as far as you know?'

'No. No drugs.'

'Are you sure?'

'Absolutely. Don't forget that I was once quite an expert on the subject.' She stepped forward.

''Bye, see you soon,' said Montalbano, running for the door, opening it and dashing out on to the landing before the cheetah could spring, grab him in her claws and eat him alive.

*

Dimora Jewellery of Montelusa – founded in 1901, as written on the old sign religiously restored on the shop-front – were the best-known jewellers in the province. They made their hundred-plus years a point of pride, and the furnishings inside were the same as they'd been a hundred years earlier. Except that now, to get inside, it was worse than entering a bank. Armoured doors, dark Kalashnikov-proof windows, uniformed security guards with revolvers so big at their sides it was scary just to look at them.

There were three salespersons, all quite distinguished: a seventyish man, another around forty, and a girl of about twenty. Apparently they'd each been expressly selected to serve the clients of their corresponding age group. So why was it the seventy-year-old who turned to speak to him, instead of the forty-year-old, as should have been his right?

'Would you like to see something in particular, sir?'

'Yes, the owner.'

'You mean Signor Arturo?'

'If he's the owner, then Signor Arturo will do.'

'And who are you, if I may ask?'

'Inspector Montalbano.'

'Please come this way.'

He followed the man into the back room, which was a very elegant little sitting room. Art-nouveau furniture. A broad staircase of black wood, covered with a dark-red runner, led to a landing where there was a massive, closed door.

'Please make yourself comfortable.' The elderly man climbed the stairs slowly, then rang a bell beside the door, which came open with a click. He went inside and closed the door behind him. Two minutes later there was another click, the door reopened, and the old man reappeared. 'You may go upstairs.'

The inspector found himself in a spacious, light-filled room. There was a large glass desk, very modern in style, with a computer on top. Two armchairs and a sofa of the kind one sees only in architectural magazines. A huge safe, the latest model, that not even a surface-to-air missile could have opened. Another safe, this one pathetic and certainly dating back to 1901, which a wet-nurse's hairpin could have opened. Arturo Dimora, a thirty-year-old who looked straight out of a fashion advertisement, stood up and held out his hand. 'I'm at your disposal, Inspector.'

'I won't waste your time. Do you know if a certain Angelo Pardo was among your clients over the last three months?'

'Just a second.' He went back behind the glass desk and fiddled with the computer. 'Yes. He bought—'

'I know what he bought. I'd like to know how he paid.'

'Just a minute. There, yes. Two cheques from the Banca Popolare di Fanara. Do you want the account number?'

15

Leaving the jeweller's, he weighed his options. What to do? Even if he left for Fanara at once, he probably wouldn't get there till after one thirty; in other words, after the bank was already closed. The best thing was to go back to Vigàta and drive to Fanara the following morning. But his anxiety to discover something important at the bank was eating him alive, and surely his nerves would keep him up all night. All at once he remembered that banks, which he scarcely frequented, also opened in the afternoon these days. The right thing was to leave at once for Fanara, head straight for the local trattoria, Da Cosma e Damiano, where he'd eaten twice and been very well served, and then, after three, make an appearance at the bank.

When he arrived at his parked car, a rather troubling thought came over him. Namely, that he had an appointment with the commissioner. It was not clear that he would make it in time. What was he going to do about it? The following: he was going to blow out Mr Commissioner's summons. The guy had done nothing but postpone the goddamned appointment day after day. Surely he was allowed to miss one? He got into the car and drove off.

✳

Going from Enzo's restaurant to Cosma and Damiano's place in Fanara was like changing continents. Asking Enzo for a dish like the rabbit *cacciatore* he was slurping down would have been like ordering pork ribs or *cotechino* at a restaurant in Abu Dhabi.

When he got up from the table, he immediately felt the need for a walk along the jetty. But since he was in Fanara there was no jetty, for the simple reason that the sea was fifty miles away. Though he'd already had a coffee in the trattoria, he decided he'd better have another at a bar beside the bank.

To the door – one of those revolving kinds with an alarm – he must have seemed obnoxious, for it reopened behind him and commanded, 'System alarm! Deposit all metal objects outside!'

The guard sitting inside a bullet-proof glass booth glanced up from a crossword puzzle and looked at him. The inspector opened a little drawer and dropped in about a pound of euro cents that were making holes in his pockets, closed it with a plastic key, and entered the tubelike door.

'System alarm!' it repeated.

It just didn't like him! That door was dead set on busting his balls! The guard was looking at him with concern. The inspector took out his house keys, put them into the drawer, went back into the door, the half-tube closed behind him, the door said nothing, but the other half of the tube, the one in front of him, didn't open. Imprisoned! The door had taken him captive, and if he wasn't freed in a few seconds he was fated to die a terrible death by suffocation. Through the glass he saw the guard engrossed in his crossword puzzle; he hadn't noticed anything. Inside the bank there wasn't a living soul to be seen. He raised his foot and gave the door a powerful kick. The guard heard the noise, realized what was happening, pushed a button on some contraption in front of him and the back half of the tube finally opened, allowing the inspector to enter the bank. Which consisted of a first entrance, with a small table and a few chairs, that led to two doors: the one on the right was an office with two vacant desks, the one on the left had the usual wood and glass partition with two tellers' windows over which were plaques saying Window 1 and Window 2, in case anyone wasn't sure. But only one had a teller behind it, and that was indeed Window 1. One could not in all conscience say that the bank did a lot of business.

'Hello, I would like to speak to the manager. I'm Inspector—'

'Montalbano!' said the fiftyish man behind the window.

The inspector gave him a puzzled look.

'Don't you remember me? Eh, don't you?' said the teller, getting up and heading towards the door at the end of the partition.

Montalbano racked his brain but couldn't come up with a name. Meanwhile the teller came straight up to him, unshaven, arms half open and ready to embrace his long-lost friend. But don't these people who expect to be recognized after forty years realize that time has done its work on their faces? That twenty winters, as the poet says, have dug deep furrows in the field of what was once adorable youth?

'You really don't remember, do you? Let me give you a little hint.'

A little hint? What was this? A TV game show?

'Cu ... Cu ...'

The inspector took a wild stab. 'Cucuzza?'

'Cumella! Giogiò Cumella!' said the other, leaping at his throat and crushing him in a python-like grip.

'Cumella! Of course!' Montalbano mumbled.

In truth he didn't remember a goddamned thing. Night and fog.

'Let's go and have a drink. We need to celebrate! *Matre santa*, it's been so many years!'

When they were passing in front of the guard's little

cage, Cumella informed him, 'Lullù, I'll be at the bar next door with my friend. If anyone comes, tell them to wait.'

But who was this Cumella? A former schoolmate? University chum? Student protester from 'sixty-eight?

'You married, Salvù?'

'No.'

'I am. Three kids, two boys and a girl. The girl, who's the youngest, is a beauty. Her name's Natasha.'

A Natasha in Fanara. Like Ashanti in Canicattì, Samantha in Fela, and Jessica in Gallotti. Didn't anybody name their little girls Maria, Giuseppina, Carmela or Francesca any more?

'What'll you have?'

'A coffee.'

At that hour, one coffee more or less made no difference.

'Me too. Why did you come to our bank, Inspector? I've seen you a couple of times on television.'

'I need some information. Perhaps the manager—'

'I'm the manager. What's this about?'

'One of your clients, Angelo Pardo, was murdered.'

'I heard.'

'I couldn't find any of your statements in his apartment.'

'He didn't want us to send them to him. And he sent us the order in a registered letter! Imagine that! He'd come and pick them up himself.'

'I see. Could you tell me how much is in his account and if he made any investments?'

'No, unless you've got a judge's authorization.'

'I haven't.'

'Then I can't tell you that until the day he died he had somewhere around eight hundred thousand.'

'Lire?' asked Montalbano, a little disappointed.

'Euros.'

That put things in a whole new light. Over a billion and a half lire.

'Investments?'

'None whatsoever. He needed ready cash.'

'Why did you specify "until the day he died"?'

'Because three days before he'd taken out a hundred thousand. And from what I've heard, if he hadn't been shot, within three days he would have made another withdrawal.'

'What have you heard?'

'That he lost it all gambling at Zizino's den.'

'Can you tell me for how long he was a client of yours?'

'Less than six months.'

'Was he ever in the red?'

'Never. Anyway, for us at the bank it wasn't a problem, no matter what happened.'

'Explain.'

'When he opened the account, he was accompanied

by MP di Cristoforo. But that's enough. Let's talk a little about old times.'

Cumella did all the talking, reminiscing about episodes and people the inspector had no recollection of. But to make it look as if he remembered everything, Montalbano had only to say, every now and then, 'Right!' and 'How could I forget?'

At the end of their conversation, they said goodbye, embracing and promising to stay in touch by telephone.

On the way back, not only was the inspector unable to enjoy the discovery he'd made but his mood turned darker and darker. The moment he got into the car and drove off, a question was buzzing about in his head like an annoying fly: how come Giogiò Cumella could remember their grammar-school days and he couldn't? From a few of the names Giogiò had mentioned, a few of the events he had recounted, elusive flashes of memory had come back to him in fits and bursts, but like pieces of an insoluble puzzle with no precise outline, and the flashes had led him to situate the time of his friendship with Cumella in their grammar-school days. Unfortunately, there could only be one answer to his question: he was beginning to lose his memory. An indisputable sign of old age. But didn't they say that old age made you forget what you did the day before and remember things from when you were a little kid? Well, apparently that wasn't always the case. Obviously there was old age and old age.

What was the name of that disease where you even forget you're alive? The one President Reagan had? What was it called? There, see? He was even starting to forget things of the present.

To distract himself, he formulated a proposition. A philosophical proposition? Maybe, but tending towards 'weak thought' – exhausted thought, in fact. He even gave this proposition a title: 'The Civilization of Today and the Ceremony of Access'. What did it mean? It meant that, today, to enter any place whatsoever – an airport, a bank, a jeweller's or watchmaker's shop – you had to submit to a specific ceremony of control. Why ceremony? Because it served no concrete purpose. A thief, a hijacker, a terrorist, if they really want to enter, will find a way. The ceremony doesn't even serve to protect the people on the other side of the entrance. So whom does it serve? It serves the very person about to enter, to make him think that, once inside, he can feel safe.

*

'Aaaah, Chief, Chief! I wannata tell you that Docter Latte with an S called! He said as how the c'mishner couldn't make it today.'

'Couldn't make what?'

'He din't tell me, Chief. But he said he can make it tomorrow, at the same time of day.'

'Fine. Getting anywhere with the file?'

'I'm almost somewhere. Right at the tip o' the tip!

Ah, I almost forgot! Judge Gommaseo also called sayin' 'at you's asposta call 'im when you get in so you can call 'im.'

He'd just sat down when Fazio came in. 'The phone company says it's not technically possible to retrace the calls you received when you were at Angelo Pardo's place. They even told me why, but I didn't understand a word of it.'

'The people who called didn't know yet that Angelo'd been shot. One of them even hung up. He wouldn't have done that if he didn't have something to hide. We'll deal with it.'

'Chief, I also wanted to mention that I don't know anybody in Fanara.'

'It doesn't matter. I worked it out myself.'

'How did you do that?'

'I knew for certain that Angelo had an account at the Banca Popolare in Fanara. So I went there. The bank manager is an old schoolmate of mine, a dear friend, and so we reminisced about the good old days of our youth.'

Another lie. But its purpose was to make Fazio believe that he still possessed an ironclad memory.

'How much did he have in the account?'

'A billion and a half old lire. And he really gambled big-time, as you told me yourself. Betting money he certainly didn't earn as a pharmaceutical representative.'

'The funeral's tomorrow morning. I've seen the announcements.'

'I want you to go.'

'Chief, it's only in movies that the killer goes to the funeral of the person he killed.'

'Don't be a wise guy. You're going anyway. And take a good look at the names on the ribbons on the wreaths and pillows.'

Fazio left, and the inspector phoned Tommaseo.

'Montalbano! What are you doing? Did you disappear?'

'I had things to do, Judge, I'm sorry.'

'Listen, I want to fill you in on something I think is really serious.'

'I'm listening.'

'A few days ago you sent Angelo Pardo's sister, Michela, to see me. Do you remember?'

'Of course.'

'Well, I've interrogated her three times. The last time just this morning. A disturbing woman, don't you think?'

'Oh, yes.'

'Something troubled about her, I'd say.'

'Oh, yes.' And you had a ball in those troubled waters, like a little pig under your august magistrate's robes.

'And what unfathomable eyes she has.'

'Oh, yes.'

'This morning she exploded.'

'In what sense?'

'In the sense that at a certain point she stood up, summoned a very strange voice, and her hair came undone. Chilling.'

So Tommaseo, too, had witnessed a bit of Greek tragedy.

'What did she say?'

'She started inveighing against another woman, Elena Sclafani, her brother's girlfriend. She claims she's the killer. Have you interrogated her?'

'Sclafani? Of course.'

'Why didn't you inform me?'

'Well, it's just that—'

'What's she like?'

'Beautiful.'

'I'm going to summon her immediately.'

How could you go so wrong? Tommaseo was going to dive into Elena like a fish.

'Look, Judge, I—'

'No, no, my dear Montalbano, no excuses. Among other things, I must tell you that Michela accused you of protecting Signora Sclafani.'

'Did she tell you why Signora Sclafani would—'

'Yes, jealousy. She also told me that you, Montalbano, have in your possession some letters Sclafani wrote in which she threatens to kill her lover. Is that true?'

'Yes.'

'I want to see them at once.'

'OK, but—'

'I repeat, no excuses. Don't you realize how you're behaving? You hid from me—'

'Don't piss outside the urinal, Tommaseo.'

'I don't understand.'

'I'll explain. I said, don't piss outside the urinal. I'm not hiding anything from you. It's just that Elena Sclafani has an alibi for the evening Pardo was killed, and it's one you're really going to like.'

'What does that mean?'

'You'll see. Make sure she goes into great detail. Have a good evening.'

✡

'Inspector Montalbano? It's Laganà.'

'Good evening, Marshal. What can you tell me?'

'That I've had a stroke of luck.'

'In what sense?'

'Last night, entirely by chance, I got wind of a huge operation that's going to be revealed to the press tomorrow. We're about to make a big sweep of more than four thousand people, including doctors, pharmacists and representatives, all accused of corruption and graft. So today I called a friend of mine in Rome. Well, it turns out the pharmaceutical firms represented by Angelo Pardo haven't been implicated.'

'That means Pardo couldn't have been killed by some rival, or for not making payoffs.'

'Exactly.'

'And what do you make of those four pages covered with numbers I gave you?'

'I turned them over to Melluso.'

'Who's he?'

'A colleague who knows all about that sort of thing. I'm hoping I'll have something to tell you tomorrow.'

*

'Aaaaaaaaaah!'

A high-pitched, piercing, prolonged yell terrorized everyone who was still at the station. It came from the entrance. With a chill passing down his spine, Montalbano rushed into the corridor, running into Fazio, Arguello, Gallo and a couple of uniformed policemen.

Inside his cubby-hole stood Catarella, back glued to the wall, no longer screaming but, rather, whimpering like a wounded animal, eyes popping out of his head, pointing with a trembling finger at Angelo Pardo's open laptop on the little table.

Matre santa! What could have appeared on the screen to frighten him so? The devil? Osama bin Laden?

'Everybody stay outside!' Montalbano ordered, going into the cubby-hole.

He looked at the monitor. It was blank. There was nothing.

Maybe Catarella's brain, having so strained itself in the struggle with the passwords, had completely melted. Which, in any case, wouldn't have taken much.

'Go away!' the inspector yelled to his men.

When he was alone with Catarella, he embraced him. Feeling him trembling, he told him to sit down. 'There's a good boy,' he murmured, stroking his head.

And, just like a dog, Catarella started to calm down. When he saw he was no longer trembling, Montalbano asked him, 'Can you tell me what happened?'

Catarella made a gesture of despair.

'Come on, try to talk. Do you want a little water?'

Catarella shook his head, 'No,' and swallowed twice.

'It – it – deleted isself, Chief,' he said, in a voice about to break into a heartrending wail.

'Come on, speak up. What deleted itself?'

'The third file, Chief. And it deleted the other two, too.'

Therefore everything that might have been of interest in the laptop had been lost.

'How is that possible?'

'Oh, iss possible, Chief. There musta been an abortion pogram.'

Abortion? Maybe Angelo Pardo, aside from performing illegal abortions on women, had also found a way to perform them on computers.

'What have abortions got to do with this?'

'Chief, whatta you say when you got a militiry operation going an' you wanna stop it?'

'I dunno, I guess you could say you abort it.'

'And in't that what I said? Iss what I said. Iss got an

abortion pogram pogrammed to delete what's asposta be deleted in the abortion pogram pogrammed to be deleted after a week, a month, two months, tree months . . . You follow?'

'Perfectly. A timed deletion program.'

'Just like you say, Chief. But iss not cause of my fault or negleck, Chief! I swear!'

'I know, Cat, I know. Don't worry about it.'

He patted Catarella's head again and went back into his office. Angelo Pardo had taken every possible precaution to make sure nobody ever found out how he'd got the money he'd needed to gamble and buy expensive gifts for his girlfriend.

16

The first thing he did when he got home was attack the salmon. A hefty slice dressed with fresh lemon juice, and a special olive oil given him by the person who had made it. ('The virginity of this olive oil has been certified by a gynaecologist,' said the little ticket that had come with it.) After eating, he cleared the veranda table and replaced the dish and cutlery with a brand-new bottle of J&B and a glass. He knew at last that he held the end of a long thread in his hand. *And if you even think of calling it Ariadne's thread, I'll slash your face*, he warned himself. But that thread might lead him, if not to a solution, at least down the right path.

It was Prosecutor Tommaseo who, without knowing it, had handed him the thread. He'd told him that during the last interrogation Michela had made a scene straight out of a Greek tragedy, screaming that he, Montalbano, didn't want to take any action against Elena even though he had in his possession the letters in which Elena had threatened to kill Angelo. And while it was absolutely true that he had those compromising letters, there was a small detail that could not be ignored: Michela should not have known this.

Because the day before, when Michela asked him if he'd found the letters, he'd said no, just to keep the waters muddy. And he remembered this perfectly clearly – forget about old age and Alzheimer's (there, that's what that disease was called!). And Paola the Red had also been present and could testify.

The only person who knew he'd found the letters was Elena, because he'd shown them to her. But the two women didn't speak. So? There was only one answer. Michela had gone to the garage to check if the envelope with the three letters was still in the Mercedes' boot, and when she saw it was gone, she'd come to the logical conclusion that the inspector had discovered and taken it.

Wait a second, Montalbano. How could Michela have known the letters were lying hidden under the mat in the boot of the Mercedes? She'd said that Angelo kept his letters in one of the desk's drawers. Angelo had no logical reason to move them out of the house and into the Mercedes in the garage – hiding them, yes, but making sure they weren't entirely hidden, so that if anyone looked with any care, they would find them. Therefore Michela must have moved them. But when? The very night Angelo was found dead when he, Montalbano, had committed the colossal blunder of leaving her alone in her brother's apartment.

Why had Michela gone through such an elaborate song and dance?

Why would someone hide something in such a way that it can be discovered as if by chance? To make the discovery seem more significant, of course. Explain yourself better, Salvo.

If he had opened the desk drawer, found the letters there and read them, everything would have seemed normal. Let's set the value of the words in those letters at ten. But if he'd found those letters after driving himself crazy looking for them, because they were hidden, it would mean that the letters were not supposed to have been read and thus the value of their words climbed to fifty. This lent weight and truth to the death threats: they were no longer the generic statements of a jealous lover.

Compliments to Michela. As an attempt to screw the hated Elena, it was brilliant. But her excessive hatred had betrayed her in front of Tommaseo. It was easy for her to enter the garage, since she had copies of all of Angelo's keys.

Wait a minute. The other night, after the dream about the bath at Michela's, something about a key had occurred to him. Whose key?

Inspector Montalbano, review everything from the start.

From the very beginning?

From the very beginning.

Can I pour myself another whisky first?

So, one fine day, Signora ('excuse me, Signorina') Michela Pardo appears at the station to tell me she's had no word of her brother Angelo for two days. She says she even went into his apartment, since she has a set of keys, but found everything in order. She comes back the same evening. We go to look at the apartment together. Everything still in order. There's no trace of any sudden departure. When we're outside the building, about to say goodbye, it occurs to her that we haven't checked the room Angelo has on the terrace, having rented both room and terrace. We go back upstairs. The glass door giving on to the terrace is locked. Michela opens it with one of her keys. The door to the little room on the terrace is also locked, but Michela tells me she doesn't have the key to this one. So I break down the door. And I find . . .

Stop right there, Montalbano. There's the rub, as Hamlet would say. This is the part of the story that doesn't make sense.

What sense is there in Michela having only the key to the terrace door, which is completely useless if not accompanied by the key to the former laundry room? If she has copies of *all* her brother's keys, she must also have the one to the room on the terrace. All the more so because Angelo used to go there to read or sunbathe, as Michela herself said. He did not go up there to be with his women. What did this mean?

He noticed his glass was empty again. He refilled it, stepped off the veranda on to the sand and, taking a sip of whisky every few steps, arrived at the water's edge. The night was dark, but it felt good. The lights of the fishing-boats on the horizon line looked like low-lying stars.

He picked up the thread of his argument. If Michela had a key to the little room, but told him she didn't, the lie meant she had wanted him, Montalbano, to break down the door and find Angelo shot dead inside. And this because she already knew that her brother's corpse was in that room. By staging the whole scene, she was trying to make herself appear, to the inspector's eyes, completely extraneous to the entire event, when in fact she was in it up to her neck.

He returned to the veranda, sat down, poured another whisky. How could things have gone?

Michela says that on that Monday Angelo phoned her to tell her that Elena would be coming over to his place that evening. Thus Michela made herself scarce. But what if, on the other hand, Angelo, seeing that Elena wasn't coming and realizing that she wasn't going to come, called his sister back and Michela went to see him? Maybe Angelo even told her he was going up to the terrace room to get some air. Then, when Michela turned up, she found her brother murdered. She's convinced it was Elena, who, having arrived late, had had a quarrel with Angelo. Especially since Angelo had wanted to have sex with the girl, which was all too clear. So she decides to play her ace to prevent Elena getting away with it.

She locks everything up, goes down into the apartment below, spends the night removing everything that might reveal anything about Angelo's shady dealings, above all the strongbox, and takes the letters down to the garage as they will serve as evidence against Elena ...

Montalbano heaved a sigh of satisfaction. Michela had had all the time she needed to take care of business before reporting her brother missing. And on the night he had let her stay in the apartment, she had probably slept soundly and happily, since she'd already done everything she needed to do. It was still a colossal blunder on his part, but without any immediate consequences.

But why was Michela so sure that Angelo was up to something shady? The answer was simple. When she had learned that her brother was giving extremely expensive presents to Elena, and when she had later found out that the money had not been taken from their joint account, she had become convinced that Angelo held a secret account somewhere with a great deal of money in it, too much for him to have earned honestly. The story Michela had told Montalbano about sales bonuses and providing for the family was a lie. The woman was too smart not to have smelled a rat.

But why had she taken away the strongbox? There was an answer to this, too. Because she hadn't managed to find where the second key was hidden, the one found by Fazio stuck to the bottom of the drawer. And then, if you really consider ...

The consideration began and ended there. Montalbano's eyes suddenly began to flutter, and his head dropped. The only thing to be taken into serious consideration was his bed.

✳

He had the misfortune to wake up a few minutes before the alarm rang. He realized Angelo Pardo's funeral was that morning. The word 'funeral' conjured up thoughts of death ... He leaped out of bed, raced into the shower, washed, shaved, had a coffee and got dressed, all with the frenetic rhythm of a Larry Semon silent film — to the point that he could practically hear the jaunty chords of a piano accompaniment — then went out of the house and finally recovered his normal rhythm as soon as he got into the car and began the drive into Vigàta.

Fazio wasn't at the station; Mimì, summoned by Liguori, had gone to Montelusa; and Catarella was mute, not having recovered from the blow dealt him the day before by Pardo's computer when all the passwords had suddenly vanished and he had been left to gaze at a monitor as empty as the fabled Tartar desert.

A morgue, in short.

✳

Around mid-morning the first phone call came in.

'My dear Inspector, the family all well?'

'Excellent, Dr Lattes.'

'Let's thank the Blessed Virgin! I wanted to tell you that unfortunately the commissioner can't see you today. Shall we make it the same time tomorrow?'

'Let's do that, Doctor.'

With thanks to the Blessed Virgin, he'd been spared the sight of the commissioner's face for yet another day. Meanwhile, however, he'd become curious to know what the man wanted to see him about. Certainly nothing important, if he kept postponing with such ease.

Let's hope he manages to tell me before I retire or he's transferred, he thought.

*

The second call came just after the first.

'It's Laganà, Inspector. My friend Melluso – I gave him those pages to decipher, remember . . . ?'

'Of course I remember. Has he succeeded in cracking the code?'

'Not yet. But meanwhile he's made a discovery that I thought could be important to your investigation.'

'Really?'

'Yes, but I'd like to tell you about it in person.'

'Suppose I call in around five thirty this afternoon?'

'Fine.'

*

The third came at half past noon.

'Montalbano? Tommaseo here.'

'What is it?'

'Elena Sclafani came in to see me at nine o'clock this morning . . . My God!'

He'd suddenly lost his breath. Montalbano was worried. 'What's wrong, sir?'

'That woman is so . . . beautiful. She's a creature of . . . of . . .'

Tommaseo was beside himself. He not only couldn't breathe he also couldn't speak.

'How did it go?'

'Splendidly!' the prosecutor said enthusiastically. 'Couldn't have gone any better!'

Logically speaking, when a prosecutor declares himself satisfied and content with an interrogation, it means the accused got the worse end of things.

'Did you find any incriminating elements?'

'You must be joking!'

So much for logic. The prosecutor was clearly leaning in Elena's favour.

'The lady showed up with Traina, the lawyer, who brought along a service-station attendant, a certain Luigi Diotisalvi.'

'The lady's alibi.'

'Exactly, Montalbano. All we can do at this point is envy Mr Diotisalvi and open our own service station in the hope that sooner or later she'll need refuelling, heh, heh, heh.'

He laughed, still stunned by Elena's appearance.

'The lady was adamant in her wish that her husband should not, under any circumstances, learn of her alibi,' the inspector reminded him.

'Of course. I made every effort to reassure her. The upshot, however, is that we're back at sea. What are we going to do, Montalbano?'

'Swim, sir.'

*

At a quarter to one, Fazio returned from the funeral.

'Were there a lot of people?'

'Enough.'

'Wreaths?'

'Nine. And only one pillow, from the mother and sister.'

'Did you take down the names on the ribbons?'

'Yes, sir. Six were unknown persons, but three were known.'

His eyes glistened, a sign that he was about to drop a bomb.

'Go on.'

'One wreath was from Senator Nicotra's family.'

'Nothing strange about that. You yourself know they were friends. The senator defended him—'

'Another was from the di Cristoforo family.'

Fazio was expecting the inspector to be surprised. He was disappointed.

'I was already aware they knew each other. It was MP

di Cristoforo who introduced Pardo to the manager of the bank in Fanara.'

'And the third wreath was from the Sinagra family. The same Sinagras we know so well,' fired Fazio.

This time Montalbano was speechless.

For the Sinagras to have come this far out into the open, Angelo Pardo must have been a dear friend indeed. Had Senator Nicotra introduced Pardo to them? And was di Cristoforo therefore part of the same clique? Di Cristoforo–Nicotra–Pardo: a triangle whose area equalled the Sinagra family?

'Did you also go to the cemetery?'

'Yes, sir. But they weren't able to bury him. They put him on ice for a few days.'

'Why?'

'The Pardos have a family tomb, Chief, but when it was time to put the coffin into the vault, they couldn't manage it. The lid of the coffin was too high so they're going to have to enlarge the hole.'

Montalbano sat there pensive. 'Do you remember how Angelo Pardo was built?' he asked.

'Yeah, Chief. About five foot ten, twelve and a half stone.'

'Perfectly normal. Do you think a body that size needs an extra large coffin?'

'No, Chief.'

'Tell me something, Fazio. Where did the funeral procession begin?'

'At Pardo's mother's place.'

'Which means they'd already brought him back to Vigàta from Montelusa.'

'Yes, sir, they did that last night.'

'Listen, can you find out the name of the undertaker?'

'I already know it, Chief. Angelo Sorrentino and Sons.'

Montalbano stared at him, his eyes like slits. 'Why do you already know it?'

'Because the whole thing didn't make any sense to me. You're not the only cop around here, Chief.'

'OK, I want you to telephone Sorrentino and ask him who was directly involved in transferring the body from Montelusa to here and then to the funeral. Summon them to my office for three o'clock this afternoon.'

✽

At Enzo's he kept to light dishes since he wouldn't have time for his customary digestive-meditative walk along the jetty to the lighthouse. While eating, he further reflected on the coincidence that there had been wreaths from the Nicotra and di Cristoforo families, which had also been recently bereaved, at Pardo's funeral. Three people who were in some way linked by friendship had died in less than a week. Wait a minute, he said to himself. It was known high and low that Senator Nicotra was a friend of Pardo's, but were Nicotra and di Cristoforo friends of each other? The more one thought about it, the more it seemed that this was perhaps not the case.

After the havoc of Mani Pulite, Nicotra had gone over to the party of the Milanese property magnate and continued his political career, still supported, however, by the Sinagra family. Di Cristoforo, a former socialist, had gone over to a centrist party opposed to Nicotra's. And on more than one occasion he had more or less openly attacked Nicotra for his relations with the Sinagras. Thus you had di Cristoforo on one side, Nicotra and the Sinagras on the other, and their only point in common was Angelo Pardo. It wasn't the triangle he had at first imagined. So, what had Angelo Pardo represented for Nicotra, and what had he represented for di Cristoforo? Theoretically speaking, if he was a friend of Nicotra's, he couldn't have been the same for di Cristoforo. And vice versa. The friend of my enemy is my enemy. Unless he does something that suits friends and enemies alike.

*

'My name is Filippu Zocco.'

'And mine is Nicola Paparella.'

'Were you the ones who brought Angelo Pardo's body from the Montelusa morgue to Vigàta?'

'Yes, sir,' they said in unison.

The two fiftyish undertakers were wearing a sort of uniform: black double-breasted jacket, black tie, black hat. They looked like a couple of stereotypical gangsters from an American movie.

'Why wouldn't the coffin fit into the vault?'

'Should I talk or should you talk?' Paparella asked Zocco.

'You talk.'

'Signora Pardo called our boss, Signor Sorrentino, to her place and they decided on the coffin and the time. Then, at seven p.m. yesterday, we went to the morgue, boxed up the body and brought 'im here, to the home of this Signora Pardo.'

'Is that your normal procedure?'

'No, sir, Inspector. It happens sometimes, but it's not normal procedure.'

'What is the normal procedure?'

'We get the body from the morgue, then take it directly to the church where the funeral's to be held.'

'Go on.'

'When we got there, the lady said the coffin looked too low. She wanted it higher.'

'And was it in fact low?'

'No, sir, Inspector. But sometimes dead people's relatives get fixated on silly things. So we took the body out of the first coffin and put it in another. But the lady didn't want it covered. She said she wanted to sit up all night, but not in front of a sealed coffin. She told us to come back next morning round seven to put the lid on.

So that's what we did. We came back this morning and put the lid on. Then at the cemetery—'

'I know what happened at the cemetery. When you went to close the coffin this morning, did you notice anything strange?'

'There was something strange that wasn't strange, Inspector.'

'I don't understand.'

'Sometimes relatives put things inside the coffin, things the dead person used to like when he was alive.'

'And in this particular case?'

'In this particular case it was almost like the dead man was sitting up.'

'What do you mean?'

'The lady had put something big under his head and shoulders. Something wrapped up in a sheet. It was kind of like she put a pillow under him.'

'One last question. Would the dead man have fitted inside the first coffin in that position?'

'No,' Zocco and Paparella said again in unison.

17

'Ah, Inspector! So punctual! Make yourself comfortable,' said Laganà.

As Montalbano was sitting down, the marshal dialled a number. 'Can you come over?' he said into the receiver.

'Well, Marshal, what have you discovered?'

'If you don't mind, I'd rather my colleague told you, since he deserves the credit.'

There was a knock at the door. Vittorio Melluso was the spit and image of William Faulkner around the time the writer had received the Nobel Prize. The same southern-gentleman's elegance, the same polite, distant smile.

'The code based on that song collection is so hard to understand precisely because it's rather elementary in conception and created for personal use.'

'I don't understand what you mean by "for personal use".'

'Inspector, normally a code is used by two or three

people to communicate with one another so that they needn't fear anyone else understanding what they say. Right?'

'Of course.'

'So they make as many copies of that code as they will need for the people who wish to exchange information. Clear?'

'Yes.'

'I think the code you found is the only copy in existence. It was used only by the person who conceived it to encrypt certain names, the ones that appear in the two lists Laganà gave me.'

'Did you manage to understand any of it?'

'Well, I think I've grasped two things. The first is that every surname corresponds to a number, the one in the left-hand column. Each number has six digits, while the names are of varying length and therefore have varying numbers of letters. This means that each digit does not correspond to a letter. There are probably some dummy digits within each number.'

'Which means?'

'Digits that serve no purpose other than to throw people off. In other words, it's a code within a code.'

'I see. And what was the second thing?'

Laganà and Melluso exchanged a very quick glance.

'You want to tell him?'

'The credit is all yours,' said Laganà.

'Inspector,' Melluso began, 'you gave us two lists. In

both of these lists, the numbers on the left, the ones that stand for names, always occur and recur in the same sequence. The numbers on the right, on the other hand, are always different. After studying them closely, I arrived at a conclusion, which is that the figures on the right in the first list indicate sums of money in euros, while the figures on the right in the second list represent quantities. When you compare, for instance, the first two numbers on the right-hand side of the two lists, you discover that there's a precise relationship between the two figures, which corresponds—'

'To the current market price,' the inspector finished.

Laganà, who hadn't taken his eyes off Montalbano for the past five minutes, laughed. 'I told you, Melluso, the inspector would get it straight away!'

Melluso nodded slightly to Montalbano in homage.

'So,' the inspector concluded, 'the first list contains the names of the clients and the sum paid by each; the second indicates the amount provided each time. There was a third list in the computer, but unfortunately it self-destructed.'

'Do you now have an idea of what it contained?' asked Laganà.

'I do. I'm sure it had the dates and the amount of merchandise the provider – let's call him the wholesaler – delivered to him.'

'Shall I continue trying to decode the names?' asked Melluso.

'Of course. I'd really appreciate it.'

He didn't say that, of those fourteen names, he already knew two.

*

When he got back to the station it was already getting dark. He picked up the telephone and rang Michela. 'Hello? Montalbano here. How are you?'

'How am I supposed to be?'

The woman's voice sounded different, as though far away, and weary, as after a long walk.

'I need to talk to you.'

'Could we put it off till tomorrow?'

'No.'

'All right, then, come over.'

'Tell you what, Michela. Let's meet in an hour at your brother's apartment, since you have the keys. All right?'

At Michela's place there were likely to be other people – the mother, the aunt from Vigàta, the aunt from Fanara, as well as friends come to offer their condolences – which might make it difficult or even impossible to talk.

'Why there of all places?'

'I'll tell you later.'

*

He raced home, undressed, slipped into the shower, put on a fresh set of clothes: underwear, shirt, socks, suit. He phoned Livia, told her he loved her, and hung up, probably leaving her befuddled. Then he poured himself a glass of whisky and went out to the veranda to drink it while smoking a cigarette. Now he had to lance the pustule, the foulest part.

*

Pulling up in front of Angelo's apartment house, he parked the car, got out and looked up at the balcony and windows on the top floor. It was pitch dark now, and he saw light in two of the windows. Michela must already have arrived. Instead of using his keys, he rang the intercom, but no voice replied. Only the click of the front door, which had been opened. He climbed the lifeless stairs of the dead building, and when he reached the top-floor landing he saw Michela waiting for him outside the door.

He was taken aback. For an ever-so-brief moment, it had seemed that the woman he was looking at was not Michela but her mother. What had happened to her?

Naturally her brother's death had been a terrible blow, but until the day before she had seemed, to Montalbano, to take it well, carrying herself intelligently and accusing forcefully. Perhaps the lugubrious funeral ceremony had finally made her aware of the definitive, irrevocable loss of Angelo. She was wearing one of her usual broad, shapeless dresses, which looked like something she'd bought at a secondhand shop where they had only sizes too large for her. It was black, for mourning, likewise the stockings and the canvas shoes, which were without heels and had a button in the middle, like nuns' shoes. She'd gathered her hair inside a big scarf, also black, of course. She stood with her shoulders hunched, leaning against the door. She kept her eyes lowered. 'Please come in.'

Montalbano entered, stopping inside the doorway. 'Where should we go?' he asked.

'Wherever you like,' replied Michela, closing the door.

The inspector chose the living room. They sat down in two armchairs facing one another. For a spell neither spoke. It was as though the inspector had come to pay his respects and stay the proper amount of time, sitting in awkward silence.

'So it's all over,' Michela said suddenly, leaning against the back of her chair and closing her eyes.

'It's not all over. The investigation is still open.'

'Yes, but it'll never be properly closed. It'll either be shelved, or you'll arrest someone who had nothing to do with it.'

'Why do you say that?'

'Because I found out Prosecutor Tommaseo didn't file any charges against Elena after interrogating her. He's taken her side. As you, too, seem to have done, Inspector.'

'It was you who first brought her up, wasn't it?'

'Yes, because I was waiting for you to do so!'

'Did you tell Tommaseo I had Elena's letters to your brother in my possession?'

'Shouldn't I have?'

'No.'

'Why not? So you could continue to keep Elena out of this?'

'No, so I could continue to keep you out of it, Michela. In telling the judge what you told him, you made a mistake. You scored an own goal.'

'Explain what you mean.'

'Certainly. I never told you I found those letters. And if I didn't tell you, how did you know I had?'

'But I'm sure you told me! In fact, I remember that Paola was here...'

Montalbano shook his head. 'No, Michela, your friend Paola, if you call on her to testify, will only confirm that on that evening, when asked explicitly by you, I denied having found those letters.'

Michela said nothing, only sank further into the armchair, her eyes still closed.

'It was you, Michela,' the inspector went on, 'who took the letters that Angelo kept in his desk, put them in a large envelope, went down to the garage and hid them under the mat in the boot of the Mercedes. But you made sure that a corner of the envelope remained visible. You wanted those letters to be found. So that I, after reading them, would wonder who might have a reason to hide them. And there could only be one answer: Elena. When you went to check and saw that the envelope was gone, you were sure I had taken the letters.'

'And when would I have done all this?' she asked, in a tense voice, newly attentive and alert.

Should he tell her his hypothesis? Perhaps it was premature. He decided instead to blame himself for something he now knew to be without importance.

'The night we found Angelo. When I let you sleep alone in this apartment, which was a big mistake.'

She relaxed. 'That's pure fantasy. You have no proof.'

'We'll discuss proof in a few minutes. As you know, I looked in vain for the strongbox Angelo used to keep in his apartment. I imagine you took that away too, Michela, on the same night you took the letters.'

'Then explain to me,' the woman said ironically, 'why I would want you to find the letters and not the strong-box.'

'Because the letters might inculpate Elena, while the contents of the strongbox would certainly have inculpated your brother.'

'And what could there have been in the strongbox that would have been so compromising, in your opinion? Money?'

'No, not money. That he kept in Fanara, at the Banca Popolare.'

He was expecting a different reaction from Michela.

At the very least, Angelo had not revealed to her that he had another account and, given their relationship, the omission was close to a betrayal.

'Oh, really?' she said, only slightly surprised.

Her indifference stank of falsehood a mile away. So Michela had known damn well that Angelo had another account. And therefore she must have known all about her brother's little side business.

'You knew nothing about this other account, correct?'

'Nothing at all. I was sure he only had the joint account. I think I even showed it to you.'

'Where, in your opinion, did the money deposited in Fanara come from?'

'Oh, it must have been productivity bonuses, incentives, extra commissions, that sort of thing. I thought he kept that money at home, but apparently he put it in the bank.'

'Did you know he gambled heavily?'

'No. Absolutely not.'

Another lie. She knew her brother had caught the bug. And in fact she limited herself to denying it. She didn't ask how Montalbano had found out, where Angelo had gambled, how much he had lost or won.

'If there was a lot of money in the account,' said Michela, 'it probably means he had a few lucky evenings at the gaming table.'

The girl fenced well. She would parry and immediately follow with a thrust, exploiting her adversary's reaction. She was ready to admit everything, so long as the real source of that money never came out.

'Let's return to the strongbox.'

'Inspector, I know nothing about that strongbox, just as I knew nothing about the account in Fanara.'

'In your opinion, what could there have been in that box?'

'I haven't the slightest idea.'

'I have,' Montalbano said quietly, as though giving no importance to the assertion.

Michela showed no interest in knowing what the inspector's idea was. 'I'm tired,' she said instead, sighing.

Montalbano felt sorry for her. For in those two words he'd felt the weight of a deep, genuine weariness, a weariness not only physical, of the body, but also of the mind, the emotions, the soul. An absolute weariness. 'I can leave, if you—'

'No, stay. The sooner we finish, the better. But I ask only one thing of you, Inspector. Don't play cat and mouse with me. At this point you've worked out many things, or so it seems to me. Ask me only precise questions, and I'll answer them as best I can.'

Montalbano couldn't tell whether she was merely trying to change strategy or asking him to bring things to a close because she couldn't bear any more.

'It'll take a little time.'

'I've got as much time as you want.'

'I'd like to start by telling you that I have a very

precise idea where the box is presently located. I could have checked before our meeting tonight and confirmed my suspicion, but I didn't.'

'Why not?'

'There's no saying I necessarily have to check. It's up to you.'

'Up to me? And where do you suspect the box is?'

'At the cemetery. Inside the coffin. Under Angelo's body.'

'Oh, come on!' she said, even attempting a little smile that must have cost her a tremendous effort.

'We're getting nowhere, Michela. If you carry on like this, I'm going to be forced to check the coffin. You know what that means? It means I'll have to request a great many authorizations, the whole affair will become official, the strongbox will be opened, and everything you've done to save your brother's good name will have been for nothing.'

It was perhaps at this moment that Michela realized the game was up. She opened her eyes and looked at him. Montalbano instinctively grabbed the arms of the easy chair as if to anchor himself. But there were no stormy seas in those eyes, just a liquid expanse, yellowish and dense, slowly moving and seeming to breathe, rising and falling. It didn't frighten him, but he had the impression that if he put his finger in that liquid, it would have been burned to the bone. Michela closed her eyes again.

'Do you also know what's inside the box?'

'Yes, Michela. Cocaine. But not only.'

'What else?'

'There must also be the substance with which Angelo mistakenly cut the last part of the cocaine, turning it, without planning to, into a deadly poison. And thereby causing the death of Nicotra, di Cristoforo and others whose secret supplier he was.'

The woman took off her scarf and shook her head, making her hair fall on to her shoulders. How did I manage not to notice before that it's so white? the inspector asked himself.

'I'm tired,' Michela repeated.

'When did Angelo first start frequenting gambling dens?'

'Last year. He went out of curiosity. And that was the beginning of the end for him. The money he earned was no longer enough. So he accepted an offer somebody made to him: to supply important clients with large quantities. Given his profession, he could travel all over the province without arousing suspicion.'

'How did you manage to discover that Angelo—'

'I didn't. He told me himself. He never kept anything from me.'

'Do you know who made him this offer?'

'I do, but I'm not going to tell you.'

'Did he also tell you he'd adulterated the last batch of cocaine?'

'No, he didn't have the courage.'

'Why not?'

'Because he did it for that slut, Elena. He needed a lot of money to buy her other gifts and keep her close. And with this new system he could double the amount of stuff they gave him and keep the difference for himself.'

'Michela, why do you hate Elena so much, but not the other women your brother went with?'

Before she answered, a painful grimace twisted her mouth. 'Angelo fell truly in love with her. It was the first time that had happened to him.'

The moment had come. Montalbano summoned inside him everything there was to summon: muscles, breath, nerves. Like a diver at the edge of the diving-board, a moment before taking the plunge. Then he jumped.

'Angelo was supposed to love only you, wasn't he?'

'Yes.'

He'd done it. Penetrating that shadowy undergrowth of intertwined roots, snakes, tarantulas, vipers' nests, wild grasses and thorny brambles had been easy. He'd had no trouble entering the dark wood. But walking through it would take courage.

'But hadn't you once been engaged? Weren't you in love?'

'Yes. But Angelo...'

There, under a tree, he'd found the malignant plant. Beautiful to look at, but put a leaf in your mouth and it's lethal.

'Angelo got rid of him. Is that right?'

'Yes.'

There was no end to this sick forest and its stench of death. The further in you went, the greater the horror you wanted neither to see nor to smell waiting in ambush.

'And when Teresa got pregnant, was it you who persuaded Angelo to make the girl abort and set a trap for her?'

'Yes.'

'Nobody was supposed to interfere with your ... your ...'

'What's wrong, Inspector?' she whispered. 'Can't find the right word? Love, Signor Montalbano. The word is love.'

She opened her eyes and looked at him. On the surface of the yellowish liquid expanse there were now large bubbles, popping as if in slow motion. Montalbano imagined the stink they gave off, a sickly sweet smell of decomposition, of rotten eggs, the miasmas of fetid swamps.

'How did you find out Angelo'd been killed?'

'I got a phone call. That same Monday around nine p.m. They told me they'd gone to talk to Angelo but had found him dead. They ordered me to remove everything that might reveal the sort of work Angelo was doing for them. And I obeyed.'

'You not only obeyed. You also went into the room where your brother had just been killed and planted false evidence against Elena. It was you who staged that whole scene of the panties in the mouth, the unbuckled jeans, his member hanging out.'

'Yes. I wanted to be sure, absolutely certain, that Elena would be charged with the crime. Because she did it. When those other people arrived, Angelo was already dead.'

'We'll see about that later. They may have lied to you, you know. For now, tell me: do you know who called you to tell you your brother was dead?'

'Yes.'

'Tell me his name.'

Michela stood up slowly. She spread her arms as though stretching. 'I'll be back in a minute,' she said, 'I need a drink of water.'

She left the room and headed for the kitchen, her shoulders more hunched than ever, feet dragging on the floor.

Montalbano didn't know how or why, but all at once he got up and ran after her. Michela wasn't there. He went out on to the balcony. A small light illuminated the area in front of the garage. But its dim glow was enough to reveal a kind of black sack, immobile, on the ground.

Michela had thrown herself down, without a word, without a cry. And the inspector realized that tragedy, when acted out in front of others, strikes poses and speaks in a loud voice, but when it is deep and true it speaks softly and makes humble gestures. There: the humility of tragedy.

He made a snap decision. He'd never gone to Angelo's apartment that evening. When the woman's body was discovered, they would think she had killed herself because she couldn't get over the loss of her brother. And that was how it should be.

He closed the door to the apartment softly, terrified that His Majesty might catch him in the act. He descended the still lifeless stairs, went outside, got into his car and drove home to Marinella.

18

The moment he entered his house he felt very tired. Great was the desire to lie down, pull the covers over his head and stay that way, eyes closed, trying to blot out the world.

It was eleven p.m. As he was taking off his jacket, tie and shirt, he managed, like a magician, to dial Augello's number.

'Salvo, are you crazy?'

'Why?'

'Calling at this hour! You'll wake the baby!'

'Did I wake him?'

'No.'

'So why are you being such a pain in the arse? I have something important to tell you. Come out to my place now.'

'But, Salvo—'

He hung up. Then he phoned Livia, but there was no answer. Maybe she'd gone to the movies. He undressed completely, went into the shower, used up all the water in the first tank, cursed the saints, was about to open the reserve tank but stopped. If they didn't deliver any water during the night, how would he wash in the morning? Better play it safe.

Waiting for Mimì, he decided to busy himself cutting his toe- and fingernails. Just as he finished, the bell rang, and he went to open the door, still naked.

'But I'm married!' said Mimì, scandalized. 'You didn't by any chance invite me over to see your butterfly collection, did you?'

Montalbano turned his back to him and went to put on a pair of underpants and a shirt.

'Will this be long?' asked Mimì.

'Fairly.'

'Then give me a whisky.'

They sat down on the veranda. Before drinking, Montalbano raised his glass. 'Congratulations, Mimì.'

'What for?'

'For solving the case of the wholesale dealer. Tomorrow you can strut your stuff for Liguori.'

'Is this some kind of joke?'

'Not at all. It's too bad they killed him, but he betrayed the trust of the Sinagra family.'

'Who?'

'Angelo Pardo.'

Augello's jaw dropped. 'The guy who was found shot with his dick hanging out?'

'The very same.'

'I was convinced it was a crime of passion. Women problems.'

'That's what they wanted us to think.'

Augello twisted up his mouth. 'Are you sure of what you're saying, Salvo? Do you have proof?'

'The proof is in a strongbox you'll find inside Angelo Pardo's coffin. Get authorization, open it, grab the strong-box, open that too – with the key that I'll give you in a second – and inside you'll find not only cocaine but the other stuff that turned it into poison.'

'Excuse me, Salvo, but who put the strongbox into the coffin?'

'His sister, Michela.'

'So she's an accomplice!'

'You're mistaken. She had no idea what her brother was up to. She thought the box – to which she didn't have a key – contained personal items of Angelo's so she put it into his coffin.'

'Why?'

'So that every now and then, in the afterlife, he could open it, look at the things inside and remember the good old days when he was alive.'

'Am I supposed to believe that?'

'You mean the story of the dead guy opening the strongbox now and then?'

'I mean the bit about his sister being unaware of her brother's dealings.'

'No. Not you. But everyone else, yes. *They* are supposed to believe it.'

'And what if Liguori interrogates her and she ends up contradicting herself?'

'Don't worry, Mimì. She won't be interrogated.'

'How can you be so sure?'

'I just am.'

'Then tell me everything, from the beginning.'

He told him almost everything, but sang only half the Mass. He didn't tell him that Michela was neck-deep in that shit, only knee-deep; he explained that Angelo's need for money came from his gambling addiction, thus leaving Elena discreetly in the shadows; and he informed him that Customs Police Marshal Laganà and a colleague of his could provide him and Liguori with a host of useful information.

'But how did Pardo come to know the Sinagra family?'

'His father was a big political supporter of Senator Nicotra. And the senator had introduced Angelo to some of the Sinagras. When the Sinagras found out that Pardo was hard up for cash, they got him to work for them. Angelo betrayed their trust, so they had him killed.'

'I thought I heard that some threads of women's panties were f—'

'Just for show, Mimì, to muddy the waters.'

They talked a little while longer. Montalbano gave

him Angelo's keys, and as Mimì was saying goodbye, the telephone rang.

'Livia, darling?' the inspector asked.

'Sorry to disappoint you, Chief.'

It was Fazio.

'I've just found out that Michela Pardo's been found dead. A suicide. Threw herself off the balcony at her brother's place. I'm at the station, but I have to go over there. Do you have the keys to the apartment?'

'Yes. I'll send them over with Inspector Augello, who happens to be here with me.'

He hung up. 'Michela Pardo committed suicide.'

'Poor thing! What'll we say? That she couldn't get over the grief?' asked Augello.

'That's what we'll say,' said Montalbano.

✳

In the four days that followed, nothing whatsoever happened. The commissioner postponed his meeting with Montalbano to a date as yet to be determined.

Elena never called either.

And that displeased him, in a way. He thought the girl had him in her sights and had put off the attack until the investigation was over. 'To avoid any misunderstand-ings', as she'd said. Or something similar.

And she was right. If she'd put her powers of seduction to work at the time, Montalbano might have thought she was doing it to gain his friendship and make him an accomplice. But now that even Tommaseo had exonerated her, there was no more possibility of misunderstanding. So?

Want to bet the cheetah had been eyeing a different prey? And it was he who had misunderstood? He was like a rabbit that sees a cheetah coming after it and starts running away in terror. All at once the rabbit no longer senses the ferocious beast behind it. It turns and sees the cheetah pursuing a fawn.

The question was this: why, instead of feeling happy, did the rabbit feel a wee bit disappointed?

*

On the fifth day Mimì arrested Gaetano Tumminello, a man from the Sinagra family suspected of four other killings, for the murder of Angelo Pardo.

For twenty-four hours Tumminello insisted he had never set foot in Angelo Pardo's apartment. Indeed he swore he didn't even know where the man had lived. The alleged murderer's photograph appeared on television. Then Commendatore Ernesto Laudadio, alias HM Victor Emmanuel III, showed up at the station to report that on that Monday evening he hadn't been able to enter his garage because there'd been a car he'd never seen before parked in front of it, whose licence-plate number he'd taken down. He'd honked his horn, and after a brief interval the owner had appeared — none other than, you guessed it, the man shown in the photo on television, there was no mistaking him, whereupon said man, without so much as saying, 'Goodnight,' had got back into his car and left.

As a result, Tumminello had to change his story. He said he'd gone to Pardo's to talk business, but had found him already dead. He knew nothing about the panties stuck in Pardo's mouth. He also stated quite specifically that when he'd seen him, the zip of Pardo's jeans was closed. So when he heard that Pardo had been found in an obscene pose (that's exactly how he put it: an 'obscene pose'), he, Tumminello, was shocked.

Nobody believed him, of course. Not only had he killed Pardo for having put lethal cocaine into circulation, risking a massacre, but he'd also tried to mislead the investigation. The Sinagras disowned him, and Tumminello, in keeping with tradition, got the Sinagras off the hook. He claimed the idea for getting into drugs was his and his alone, just like the idea to enlist the help of Angelo Pardo, whom he had known was short of cash, and that, of course, the Family who had honoured him by taking him in, as if he were a devoted and respectful son, was entirely in the dark about all this. He repeated, however, that when he'd gone to talk to Pardo about the huge fuck-up he'd made in cutting the cocaine, he'd found him already dead.

'Isn't saying you went to talk to him a polite euphemism for saying you'd gone to see Pardo to kill him?' the prosecutor had asked.

Tumminello did not answer.

Meanwhile Marshal Melluso, Laganà's colleague, had managed to decipher Angelo's code, and the nine people on his list found themselves in a pretty pickle. Actually there were fourteen names, not nine, but the other five (including the engineer Fasulo, Senator Nicotra and the honourable di Cristoforo) belonged to people who, thanks to Angelo Pardo's modest talents in chemistry, could no longer be prosecuted.

✳

A week later, Livia came to spend three days in Vigàta. They didn't quarrel even once. On Monday morning, at the crack of dawn, Montalbano drove her to Punta Raisi airport and, after watching her leave, got into the car to drive back to Vigàta. Since he had nothing else to do, he decide to take a back road the whole way, one in pretty bad shape, yes, but it allowed him to enjoy for a few miles the landscape he loved, made up of parched terrain and little white houses. He rolled along for three hours, head emptied of thoughts. All at once he realized he was on the road leading from Giardina to Vigàta, meaning that he was only a few miles from home. Giardina? Wasn't this the road with the service station where Elena, that Monday evening, had made love to the attendant? What was his name? Ah, yes, Luigi.

'Let's go and meet this Luigi,' he said to himself.

He drove even more slowly than before, looking left and right. At last he found the station. A little platform roof, half crowned by lighted fluorescent tubes under which stood three pumps. That was all. He pulled in and stopped. The attendant's shelter was made of brick and almost entirely hidden by the trunk of a thousand-year-old Saracen olive tree. It was almost impossible to spot it from the road. The door was closed. He hooted, but nobody came out. What was the problem? He got out of the car and went to knock at the door of the shelter. Nothing. Silence. Turning to go back to the car, he noticed, at the very edge of the space at the side of the road, the back of a metal rectangle supported by an iron bar. A sign. He went to the front but couldn't read it because three-quarters of it was covered with a clump of weeds, which he proceeded to beat down with his feet. The sign had long lost its paint and was spotted with rust, but the words were still clear: CLOSED MONDAYS.

Once, when he was a kid, his father, just to tease him, had told him the moon was made of paper. And since he had never doubted what his father said, he believed it. Now, as a mature, experienced man with brains and intuition, he had once again, like a little kid, believed what two women, one dead and the other alive, had said when they told him the moon was made of paper.

*

The rage so clouded his vision that, first, he nearly ran over a little old lady and then he barely escaped colliding with a truck. When he pulled up in front of Elena's place, it was past one o'clock. He rang the intercom and she answered.

She was waiting for him in the doorway, wearing gym clothes and smiling. 'Salvo, what a pleasant surprise! Come on in and make yourself at home.'

She went in first. From behind, Montalbano noticed that her gait was no longer springy and taut but soft and relaxed. Even the way she sat down in the armchair was almost languid, nonchalant. Apparently the cheetah had recently had her fill of fresh flesh and for the moment presented no danger. It was better this way.

'You didn't forewarn me so I haven't made coffee. But it'll only take a second.'

'No, thanks. I need to talk to you.'

Still the wild animal, she bared her sharp white teeth in a cross between a smile and a feline hiss. 'About us?'

She was clearly trying to provoke him, but only in jest, without serious intent.

'No, about the investigation.'

'Still?'

'Yes. I need to talk to you about your false alibi.'

'False? Why false?'

Only curiosity, almost as though amused. No embarrassment, surprise, fear.

'Because on that fateful Monday evening, you could not have met your Luigi.'

That 'your' he tossed in had escaped him. Apparently he still felt a twinge of jealousy. She understood and threw fuel on the fire. 'I assure you I did meet him, and we rather enjoyed ourselves.'

'I don't doubt that, but it wasn't on a Monday because that filling station is closed on Mondays.'

Elena folded her hands, raised her arms over her head and stretched. 'When did you find out?'

'A few hours ago.'

'Luigi and I could have sworn it would never occur to anyone to check.'

'It occurred to me.'

A lie. Said not to boast, but to avoid looking like a complete nincompoop in her eyes.

'A bit late, however, Inspector. Anyway, what difference does this great discovery make?'

'It means you don't have an alibi.'

'Ouf! Didn't I already tell you I had no alibi? Have you forgotten? I didn't try to make anything up. But you kept insisting, "Careful, if you don't have an alibi, you're going to be arrested!" What do you want from me? In the end I got my alibi, just as you wanted.'

Shrewd, alert, intelligent, beautiful. Stray just an inch,

and she'll take advantage. So now it was his fault that she'd lied to Tommaseo!

'How did you persuade Luigi? By promising to sleep with him?'

He couldn't control himself. The thorn of jealousy was making him say the wrong things. The rabbit couldn't accept being refused by the cheetah.

'Wrong, Inspector. Everything that I said happened to me on Monday actually happened to me the day before, on Sunday. It didn't take much to persuade Luigi to move our first encounter up one day when he talked to Tommaseo. And I can tell you that, if you want to interrogate him, he'll continue to swear blind that we met for the first time that goddamned Monday evening. He'd do anything for me.'

What was it that made his ears perk? Some small detail, perhaps, some unexpected change in her tone when she said 'that goddamned Monday evening' had suddenly, in a flash, brought something to mind — an idea, an illumination that nearly frightened him.

'You, that evening, went to Angelo's,' the inspector's mouth said, before the idea had fully taken concrete form in his head.

Not a question, but a clear assertion. She shifted position, rested her elbows on her knees, put her head into her hands and eyed Montalbano long and hard. She was studying him. Under that stare, which was weighing his value as a man, brains and balls included, the inspector felt the same unease as when he'd undergone his army physical, standing naked in front of the commission as the doctor measured and manhandled him. Then she made up her mind. Perhaps he'd passed the test.

'You realize I could stick to my story and nobody could ever prove it was false.'

'That's what you think. The sign is still there.'

'Yes, but getting rid of it would have made things worse. That was what Luigi and I decided. He'll just say he forgot a book in the booth and went back to get it that Monday evening. He's working for exams at the university. I saw him at the service station and mistakenly thought he was closing. You know the rest. Does it work?'

Damned woman! It worked, all right! 'Yes,' he said reluctantly.

'So I can go on. You're right, Inspector. That Monday evening, after driving around in the car for a couple of hours, I went to Angelo's place, very late for our appointment.'

'Why?'

'I'd decided to tell him once and for all that it was over between us. What had happened the day before with Luigi had convinced me that I no longer felt anything for Angelo. So I went to see him.'

'How did you get in?'

'I rang the intercom. There's an intercom in the terrace room, too. He answered, buzzed me in and told me to come upstairs. When I got there, he kept dialling a number on his mobile phone. He explained that when he'd thought I wasn't coming after all, he'd rung Michela and told her to come and see him. Now he wanted to warn her that I was there and that it was therefore better if she didn't. But he couldn't get hold of her. Maybe Michela had turned off her phone. Then he said, "Shall we go downstairs?" He wanted to make love, Michela or no Michela. I said no, I'd come to break up with him. That triggered a big long scene, with him crying and begging. He even got down on his knees and implored me. At one point he suggested we go away and live together, screaming he couldn't take any more of Michela and her jealousy. He said she was a leech, a parasite. Then he tried to embrace me. I pushed him and he fell into the armchair. I took advantage of this and left. I couldn't stand it any longer. And that was the last time I saw Angelo. Satisfied?'

While telling her story, her pout had increased, and her eyes had turned a dark, almost gloomy blue.

'So, to conclude your story, it was Tumminello who killed Angelo.'

'I don't think so.'

Montalbano leaped out of his armchair. What was going through Elena's head? Wasn't it to her advantage to fall in with public opinion and blame the *mafioso*? Of course it was. So why was she casting doubt on the whole affair? What was driving her to speak? Apparently she couldn't restrain her own nature.

'I don't think it was him,' she reiterated.

'So who was it?'

'Michela. Don't you realize, Inspector, the kind of relationship those two had? They were in love — at least, they were until Angelo fell in love with me. When I left the room, I thought I saw something move in the darkness on the terrace. A shadow moving very fast. I think it was Michela. She didn't get Angelo's phone call and had come to see him. And she'd heard him weeping and saying those terrible things about her ... I think she went down to the apartment, grabbed the revolver and waited for me to leave.'

'We didn't find any weapons in Angelo's place.'

'So what? She probably took it away with her and got rid of it. But Angelo did own a revolver, which he kept in the drawer of his bedside table. He showed it to me once, saying he'd found it by accident after his father's death. Anyway, why do you think Michela killed herself?'

Montalbano suddenly remembered the sheet of stamped paper declaring that a firearm had been found. He'd seen it in a drawer of Angelo's desk and thought it of no importance. And yet it was indeed important, because it corroborated exactly what Elena had just told him and showed that the moon was no longer made of paper. The girl was now telling him the truth.

'So, is the interrogation over? Shall I make you that coffee?' she asked.

He looked at her. She looked back. The colour of her iris had now turned light blue, and her lips opened into a smile. Her eyes were a sky in early summer, a clear, open sky reflecting the changes of the day. Now and then a little white cloud would pass, ever so small, but the slightest breeze sufficed to make it vanish at once.

'Why not?' said Montalbano.

Author's Note

This is the usual disclaimer that by now I'm getting tired of stating: I made this whole story up. And therefore all the characters (along with their names and surnames), and the situations they find themselves in, belong to the realm of fantasy. Any resemblance to real people and situations is purely coincidental.

A.C.

Notes

page 5 – **'You's a doctor but not o' the medical variety'** – To rise to Montalbano's rank of *commissario*, one must have a university degree, which in Italy makes one a *dottore*.

page 35 – **the corpse was truly distinguished** – In Italian journalistic jargon, when a prominent figure, especially political, is found dead in suspicious circumstances, he or she is called a *cadavere eccellente*, or 'distinguished corpse'.

page 35 – **the old Christian Democratic party** – The Democrazia Cristiana was the ruling party of Italy from the post-Second World War era until its fall from grace and eventual disbandment in the wake of the Mani Pulite scandal in the 1990s.

page 36 – **'Clean Hands'** – English for Mani Pulite, a nationwide judicial and police investigation in the early 1990s into the endemic corruption eroding the Italian political system as well as the vast web of collusion between certain politicians, business leaders, intelligence organizations, organized crime and extremist right-wing groups. After a rash of indictments of political and business leaders, and even a few suicides, Mani

Pulite ultimately led to the demise and dissolution of the Christian Democratic party, which had governed Italy since the end of the Second World War. The Italian Socialist and Social Democratic parties were also dissolved due to the scandal, then reconstituted in other formations.

page 36 – **Milanese property speculator-cum-owner-of-the-top-three-private-nationwide-television-stations-cum-parlia-mentary-deputy, head of his own personal political party, and finally prime minister** – A reference to Silvio Berlusconi, whose Forza Italia party not only reversed many of the legal reforms instituted during the Mani Pulite scandal, but also resuscitated and rehabilitated many disgraced politicians formerly of the Christian Democratic party.

page 73 – **'Let's drop the Campanile dialogue'** – A reference to Achille Campanile (1899–1977), a popular journalist, comic playwright and humorist famous for his surreal dialogues and wordplay.

page 75 – **cornuto** – Italian for 'cuckold', *cornuto* is a common insult throughout the country, but a special favourite among southerners, Sicilians in particular.

page 95 – **Everyone knew, of course, that the last of the Savoys were notoriously trigger happy** – In 1978, when his rubber dinghy was accidentally taken from the docks after a violent storm off Corsica, Vittorio Emanuele IV, banished heir to the throne of Italy and son of the monarch here parodied, carelessly shot at a man on the yacht to which the dinghy had been attached. He missed his target, but mortally wounded Dirk Hamer, a young German who had been sleeping below deck.

page 117 – **wasn't a guy named Luigi Pirandello from around there?** – Luigi Pirandello (1867–1936), the celebrated Italian playwright, novelist and short-story writer, and 1934 Nobel Laureate, was from the Sicilian town of Agrigento, Camilleri's model for the fictional town of Montelusa.

page 132 – **others will accuse us of acting like the judges in Milan, all Communists seeking to destroy the system** – A common tactic used by Silvio Berlusconi, and other politicians of his stripe, to turn the public against the judges seeking to clean up the corruption endemic to the Italian political class was to accuse the prosecuting magistrates of being Communists motivated by ideological fervour, an accusation with no basis in fact.

page 133 – **Like the coffee they gave Pisciotta and Sindona** – Gaspare Pisciotta (1924–54) was an associate of Sicilian separatist rebel bandit Salvatore Giuliano, whom he claimed to have ultimately killed, contradicting the official version of Giuliano's death. After committal to life imprisonment, Pisciotta became violently ill after drinking coffee one morning, and died forty minutes later. An autopsy showed the cause of death to be strychnine poisoning. Michele Sindona (1920–86) was a banker with ties to the Mafia and the political underworld, as well as a history of unethical business practices. Convicted of a host of offences, including fraud, perjury and murder, he, too, was poisoned in his prison cell.

page 138 – **Three thousand lire** – At the time worth about 80p.

page 144 – **a poet once said:** – The poet is Attilio Bertolucci (1911–2000), father of the filmmaker Bernardo Bertolucci.

page 158 – **The total came to 596,000. Not much if it was in**

lire – At the time of conversion to the euro, 596,000 lire was worth about £190.

page 165 – **From Sweden with love. Ingrid** – A good friend of the inspector, Ingrid Sjostrom, a Swede married to a Sicilian and living in Vigàta, features in several other books in this series.

page 172 – **the 'Clean Hands' judges** – See notes to pages 27 and 132.

page 183 – **Dacter Arquaraquà** – Catarella's mangling of Dr Arquà's name suggests the Sicilian term *quaquaraquà*, which variously means 'worthless individual', 'blabbermouth' and 'squealer' or 'informant'.

page 183 – **The tombs shall open, the dead shall rise** – A line from the Italian national anthem, often quoted ironically to express astonishment at the occurrence of an unusual event.

page 187 – **TV movies** – In English in the original text.

page 194 – **Boccadasse** – The suburb of Genoa where Livia, Inspector Montalbano's girlfriend, lives.

page 200 – **to play the fool to avoid going to war** – *Fa u fissa pi nun iri a la guerra.* A Sicilian-Calabrian expression that essentially means to 'play dumb', i.e., to feign ignorance.

page 210 – *cotechino* – A large pork sausage served in slices.

page 216 – **'weak thought'** – *Il pensiero debole* (weak thought) is a fundamental tenet of the philosophy of post-modern Italian thinker Gianni Vattimo (born 1936), for whom it is a counterweight to such forms of *pensiero forte* (strong thought) as Christianity, Marxism and other ideological systems, and intended to overcome the violent clashes and intolerance often associated with such.

page 251 – **the dark wood** – The original Italian is '*selva oscura*', a direct quote from the opening of Dante's *Inferno*.

Notes by Stephen Sartarelli